DUKKHA

MARTIN HYDE

Blackness.

No shape or silhouette. Just the angry static of my visual system.

Where am I now?

The ground's hard beneath me. Cold. I'm naked. They took my robes.

I try to sit up, but the cuff stops my ankle, scrapes against bone, and I fall back. Try again with my foot in place. Feel around.

Brickwork. A metal ring in it a few inches from the ground. A handcuff shackling me to it.

If I shift along to the right, I can just brush the adjacent wall with my fingertips. Can't reach anything but floor and wall in any direction. Even with my free foot.

Where the fuck am I?

Can't see a thing.

There are no windows. Not even a hint of light through curtains, under a garage door. Musty, stale air.

Must be a basement.

I pull at the chain again. The cuffs are definitely locked. Clap. Clap. Listen for the echo. The room's bigger than I thought, but not huge. Yes, a basement.

But whereabouts? Still in London?

What are they going to do with me?

What do they want? I don't know them. Felt like they knew me though. Didn't feel random. The older one. Did he say my name?

Pushing me in the back of the car. Raging eyes beneath

the balaclava as he blasted me in the face with the aerosol. So angry. The can hissing and hissing and I tried to cover my eyes but they burned like acid and then that sickening feeling in my stomach and my head and that chemical smell and everything loud and immediate but then faint and distant.

Wasn't there something else? Jesus, I can't remember shit.

What have I done to deserve this? I turned my life around. I came back to help people, to serve the sangha, to serve the community. And now I'm chained to a fucking wall God knows where because of them.

A sedative after-wave rolls through me. My body heavy and aching. Muscles trembling, yearning to give out, but I grit my teeth and watch my frantic breath until it slowly subsides.

Do they want ransom? Who would they even go to? The Buddhist centre? Mum?

Why me? Why now just as I'm settling back into my new life?

Sounds like kamma to me.

Whoever they are, they're not good people. Even took my clothes. Sitting here on the ground chained to a wall.

'Hey… Hey!'

Nothing.

Motherfuckers.

Where are they now? How long was I out?

Why now?

I'm panicking. Thoughts so loud in this silence. Lost in them.

Come back to awareness. Let it pass.

Breathe. Relax.

But how am I supposed to relax when at any moment they might come in to deal with me? Or worse still, they might never come. Leave me to die here. If things remain as they are right now with no intervention, I'll waste away here in the darkness.

Dehydration will get me. Or shock. Go out seizing like an epileptic on this cold, hard ground.

They'll come back. If they wanted me dead, they'd have done it already. Probably.

My bladder clenches. Need to go soon. But not yet.

I've got nothing to hide. I'm a peaceful monk just returned to London, and I'll smile through the panic and discomfort they've put me through, and they'll see I'm no harm. And then they'll do whatever they have planned for me. Interrogate me, extort money. They can take whatever they want. Possessions and wealth don't mean much to me anymore. I just need my freedom. I need my new life back.

It's not about the money.

This is crazy. Is this really happening? I'm not dreaming or something? Feels like a dream. Or a bad acid trip.

It always does. You never actually expect reality.

The bladder bell rings, louder.

God. Where to go?

In the corner. Unless I want to lie in my own piss.

I feel along the wall, find the corner, the cuff holding my ankle back, kneel, aim my dick into the corner and piss, streaming, streaming. Raining on the tile. The smell wafts back from the walls, fills my nostrils. I shake off and crawl back to my spot. Where I came to. Where I was born into this new life.

Can sort of awkwardly lean against the wall with my shoulder. Better the other way, but my foot's still trapped under me, can't get my back against the wall.

The door must be on the other side of the room somewhere. Listen. Only silence from the room and beyond. My own heavy breathing.

Need to calm down.

I'm exhausted. Need to sleep but I'm too wide awake.

When will they come? Will I get to sleep first? Don't think I could. Not unless I was completely desperate. Too risky.

My foot starts to cramp so I shift back, sit cross-legged

facing the wall.

I shiver.

They want me to suffer. What kind of psychopaths am I dealing with?

And why me of all people?

Whywhywhy.

But you know why. Don't you, Sam?

'Got a light?'

'Yeah. Somewhere.' I check my pockets, hand her one.

'Thanks. Ooh, is that a joint?'

'Yeah, you want some?'

I offer her the joint and she hits it, exhales slowly, passes it back.

'Thanks man. So how do you know El?'

'Oh, she's on my course. We sit in lectures together sometimes.'

'Nice. And you sell her weed obviously.' She gestures to the joint.

'Well, I try to keep that on the down-low, but yeah. What about you? How you know Ella?'

'Oh, we go way back. We've known each other since like primary school. Lauren as well.' She waves to the window.

'Wow. That's quite a while. I don't think I'm in touch with anyone from back then.'

'Yeah, we have a really good relationship. They're my gals, you know.' Watching my joint. I pass it to her and she breaks from her cigarette to hit it.

'So what do you do with yourself? You go uni or work or?'

'Yeah, I work at a pet shop. It's cool. I wanted to go to uni, but um I had a bit of a breakdown and kind of fluffed my A-levels, so I've just been working. But it's fine. I'm concentrating on my art. And this way I don't have assignment deadlines to stress over.'

'I'm jealous. That's cool though. What kind of art you do?'

She passes the joint back. 'Well, I mostly do quite trippy stuff. I like to blend patterns into natural landscapes, some local places but anywhere really. I like doing animals and people as well but I'm not very good at those.'

'Wow, sounds amazing. You on socials? Where can I see your stuff?'

'Oh, yeah, I'm on Instagram. I don't post that often, but there's a bunch of my stuff on there.'

She pulls it up on her phone and shows me. A psychedelic waterfall of light, the landscape just as alive as the water. Ancient eyes staring from rocks and trees and clouds. A coastal scene where the cave, boulders, and branches make it look almost like a face. There's a name for that. Para-something.

A couple sketches of faces she swipes through. Zebras drinking from a sacred pool. Face of a Goddess in the ripples. Vague deities in the clouds.

'But yeah.' She locks her phone and puts it away.

'They're amazing. Some of them have a very Alex Grey vibe.'

'Oh, man, I love Alex Grey.'

'Yeah, he's incredible. I have a signed print of his on my wall.'

'No way. Which one?'

'It's called Theologue. Like the guy meditating with the chakras and energy systems.'

'Yeah yeah, I know the one. Nice. Do you meditate yourself?'

'I do. Not as much as I should these days. I want to go on retreat sometime, but it's finding the right time around uni and getting someone to cover my job, and I should probably take a T-break cause I won't be able to smoke there. My mum's much better with it. She meditates like every single day, even with the crazy hours she works.'

'Oh wow. Good for her. What does she do?'

'She's a paediatric nurse. But yeah, she was a bit of a hippy back in the day. Still is I guess.'

'No, that's great. Sounds like a wonderful woman.'

'Yeah. What about you? You meditate?'

'Yeah. I mean not every day. But I try to do it a couple of times a week at least. I always find when I start getting low or anxious about stuff, it's when I haven't meditated in a while. Sometimes I can sit for hours and experience things most people wouldn't even believe are possible.'

'Oh yeah? What's the longest you've sat for?'

'I don't know. You lose track of time like that, but about two or three hours I think.'

'Jesus. I don't know how you do that. I can barely sit still for half an hour. And everything starts to ache and hurt.'

'Yeah, the pain can get pretty bad, but it's just knowing like it's in your mind, and you can forget it easily when your mind moves on.'

'So what do you experience in these deeper meditation states?'

'Oh, man. Well, often I'll start to go kinda numb and then my perception of my body sort of dissolves and with it my sense of self, and my thoughts slow down and I feel kind of floaty like I'm not even located anymore. And then you can get like weird dream imagery and sounds. And it almost feels like the start of a dream. And sometimes I get this thing where my body feels like really small but really big at the same time and sounds get really loud but also far away and faint.'

'Like the beginning of *Alice in Wonderland*.'

'Yeah, something like that. But just in the darkness. It usually goes away when I open my eyes.'

'Sounds cool. I've experienced similar things with er… certain substances. But I'll have to try a longer sit sometime and see what happens.'

'Yeah man. Do it. It'll change your life.'

The windows go dark as we enter another tunnel and the guy comes on the tannoy to say we're now approaching King's Cross.

The man a few seats down jumps up and heads for the door like his life depends on it. People start to collect their things, shrug into coats, lift cases down from the overheads.

Rich calmly folds his book with a lingering half-smile.

We burst out of the tunnel again and it's cranes on the skyline, new towers in development amidst the familiar skyscrapers. Nearly three years it's been, and London's changed, always changing, but at the same time most of it's just as I left it.

And then it's black again and the wind sucks along the tunnel and the train jostles us slightly on its imperfect rails.

What if I haven't changed? What if all the training of my mind is just a facade to hide behind and I'm still the lost, broken soul I was back then?

You're not. You're different. Of course you're different. And you're not alone anymore. You have Rich. You have the sangha.

He's still holding the book between praying hands. Amidst the scattered words tattooed on the backs of his hands, the word sati stands out.

Yes, be with awareness, Sam. Not with thought. Not with feeling. Not with the heart pumping in your ears. All just transient appearances in the mind.

Out of the tunnel and approaching the station now. Screech of un-oiled brakes as the train slows.

People queue to depart the second the doors open. And then they'll race up the platform, lugging holdalls and suitcases onto other trains or into taxis, to their high-rise offices and important engagements and everything moving at a million miles an hour and not a second to waste.

Rich catches my eye and gives me a knowing smile.

If only they knew. If only they knew that there was another way. That they could stop for a minute and exhale and just be.

But we can't all be monks. Spend our lives meditating. Someone has to balance books and build infrastructure and make sure the trains run on time. Or not.

You think you're better than them? You've done worse than most of them. Enough sin for at least one lifetime. Being mindful for fifteen hours a day doesn't change who you are.

It's too soon, isn't it? I'm not ready. I shouldn't have agreed to come back with Rich.

But I came here to serve. We've been over this. A hermit hiding away in a monastery is no good to anyone but himself. And what good is that? To serve the world to my fullest, I have to exist in the world. I'll mostly be in the Buddhist centre or at home anyway. It's not like I'll be running with old friends, partying and pushing twenty bags.

But still. There are associations. Memories to deal with. Everything's connected. Does physical space have a karmic element to it?

The platform slows to a stop. The doors hiss open and the passengers flock out. We get to our feet and join the end of the queue.

Our robes draw a few more stares in the station, but most people are too busy and self-engrossed to spare a second glance. Sleepwalking. He leads us to the departure screens, scans them for his train, then nods.

'Platform twelve. And you?'

'I'll get the tube.'

'Okay. Well, I'll see you here. Welcome home, Sam.' He opens his arms and we hug.

'Thanks.' I shiver. 'I'll see you tomorrow then.'

'Yes. Take care, Sam.'

He heads for his platform, and I follow the current to the tube.

Packed in with so many bodies. The train whistling as it speeds down the tunnel.

I keep my eyes down to avoid roaming gazes. Questioning looks. A guy talks on the phone. Music spills from headphones. A couple of women giggle further down the carriage.

Everything was so quiet and spacious for so long and now my world's compressed into cramped carriages and tunnels. A second, mechanical body ferrying me to my new fate.

You've ridden the tube a thousand times. What's the problem? When did you get so damn sensitive?

He always was.

It's fine. It just feels different. I'll get used to it again in a couple of days. It's because it's the first time in years. That's what people do. They adapt.

At Green Park I change tubes. Watch the city go by. These same streets that haven't changed a bit. I hope I don't see anyone I know. For a while at least. Until I'm settled back in. They'll balk at the sight of me in robes. But what do I care? Let them stare and laugh and gossip.

Need to find a job and get a place closer to the centre. But we'll worry about that later. It'll be fine with Mum for a little while.

Still another half hour on the train.

God, I'm tired. I've only meditated and travelled today, but I guess the excitement and all the sensations I'm not accustomed to anymore have drained me. I'll sit with Mum and catch up for a bit, then get an early night. Be well rested for the centre tomorrow. My new second home for the foreseeable future.

Everything's okay. This stress here, this knot in you does no good.

Yes, when you look, there's really no problem to solve. Just changing phenomena in this open space of awareness.

Emotion, no matter how intense, only appears, changes, passes away. Same with thoughts. Sensations.

My eyes close.

Exhale.

I knock on the door. Mum's voice from inside. She wrenches the door open and pulls me into a hug.

'Oh, it's so good to have you back, Sam.'

She holds me out and examines me, lingers on my head, my face. This strange specimen who was once her son.

'My God, look at you. You look different. Older.'

'Yeah, that's how time works.'

She smiles, swats me on the shoulder. 'You know what I mean. Come on. Come in then.'

I drop my bag by the stairs and follow her into the kitchen.

'Sit sit. You want a cuppa?'

'Sure. Please.'

Something's different in here. She hasn't redecorated or replaced anything, has she? But then what is it?

Is it the clock? Did we always have that clock? It looks like it belongs here, but I can't place it. It's not even on time, is it?

No, it is. My phone shows 5:20 too.

'I've missed you, you know?'

'I missed you too. But I'm here to stay. For a while at least.'

She smiles. 'I'm glad to hear.' She makes the tea. Sets the mugs down and sits across the table from me.

'The table. You made it smaller.'

'Oh, yeah, I liked the extra space in here, and seeing as it was just me, it didn't make sense to have the big table. But I can change it back if you want.'

'I don't mind. It's fine like this, more spacious.'

'Yeah. Unless you want to have people round here. Then you'll need the bigger table. I was thinking you might want to have like a coming home party or something.'

'Oh, I don't know about that. I mean I might touch base with a couple of people after I'm settled in, but it wouldn't do me good to associate with all those people at the moment. I just want to stick with the sangha for a while.'

'Oh yeah. Fair enough. So go on. How was it? Are you enlightened yet?' She smiles.

'If only. But it was good. I needed it. But I think I'm ready to be back in the world, or at least have one foot back in it with the other in the sangha.'

'Sounds good to me. I'm really impressed you managed to meditate so much. It's one thing doing it for ten minutes or even an hour, but to do it all day every day for that long.' She examines me again, like I'm just slightly alien. 'I don't know how you do it.'

'Well, it's not that bad once you get used to it. We did a mix of walking meditation and sitting, and then service. I helped in the kitchen and in the garden sometimes. And we had regular dhamma talks from some incredible teachers. And when I wasn't on silent retreat, we talked. About Buddhism. And our lives back home. They're a really interesting bunch of people, you know.'

'I'm sure. Hey, you hungry? I was thinking of making shepherd's pie if you fancy. And there's crumble in the fridge for later.'

'Yeah, sounds good. I'm just gonna unpack my things, maybe take a shower, and then I'll come down and help if you need it.'

'Oh, don't worry about that. You make yourself at home.'

She smiles, looks like she wants to hug me again but doesn't.

My room's just as I left it. Although maybe she's hoovered and washed the sheets. I was never this tidy. It was just the manic purging of the room before I left. Removing any trace of evidence.

Alex Grey's Theologue sits meditating in his frame. My gaming monitor. Dusty guitars on the rack. Mandala tapestry above the bed.

She was here.

Phantoms sit smoking in my desk chair, cross-legged on my bed, pace in front of the window.

I empty my bag, transfer my spare robes to the laundry basket, my texts to the bedside table.

I'll need to get some new clothes. I'll be wearing robes most of the time, but I'll need some normal clothes as well.

Something nice but plain. Most of my old clothes won't suit me now.

What have we got? Hoodies and band t-shirts mostly, loud and vulgar graphics, some expensive designer pieces. And all the trainers. Can't wear any of this. Was this really who I was?

Maybe it'll help, creating a new persona for myself. I've got a little money in the bank still, and there's the stash buried down the side of the house. The emergency cash. I'll have to get a job before I start spending substantial money. But what do I need to spend money on? I'm not attached to material things like that anymore. Just rent, clothes, food. A few books to occupy myself in the evenings. I can live minimally without the old indulgences, but not a pauper or ascetic either.

The middle way.

You're getting distracted. You were going to have a shower.

I was. I'm not being very mindful. Thoughts coming too quickly. It's the environment. Just being back here with all the old associations and conditions. Already it's different from the monastery. I'm going to have to really work to stay mindful here.

It'll be easier when I get a job and a new place. A clean slate without all the triggers.

And there you go again. Grasping and aversion.

Okay, just breathe. Take a few minutes.

I fold a towel on the floor and sit to meditate.

Watch the breath. Calm. The breath and only the breath. Inhale.

Exhale.

I was just forgetting. Identifying with thought.

Yes.

Inhale.

I just need to be more vigilant with my mind. Then I won't get lost.

I.

I. I. I. I. I.
Yes. I know.
Inhale.
Exhale.
Inhale….

…Exhale. I roll onto my right shoulder, but it buys me only a few seconds' reprieve before the hard ground starts working its way back into my tissue.

Fucking cunts. How long has it been now?

Is that helpful?

No, but what am I supposed to do? How am I supposed to be calm in all of this?

If only it were some setup by Rich or one of the sangha, just the extreme, unconventional methods of some great guru.

Did you stay with awareness even in your lowest moments? Or did you panic and lose yourself in thought every second of it? Who are you really?

Yeah, maybe in some far corner of Thailand or Sri Lanka but not in the middle of London.

Not this.

My neck's starting to hurt too. Maybe I should lie on my back.

With my hands on my chest, I watch my breath. Rising. Falling. Rising. Falling.

Calm. Just be still for a moment.

What choice do I have?

A noise. The other side of the door.

I open my eyes to just another shade of black. Listen. Listen.

The lock turns over. Creak of the handle.

I push myself to my seat, feel for the wall.

The light switch snaps. The room glares at me, the pixelated, still rendering basement. He stands in the doorway, still wearing a bally.

I blink the static away and turn, pinch my dick between

my legs to hide my shame and get my back as much to the wall as I can.

Like it'd help.

You're powerless.

He disappears again, up a few steps, then reappears with a big black box. He carries it against his chest to the wall and sets it down by the shelving units. Goes back to the stairs and brings a second box, plugs them in. Not boxes. Speakers.

'Hey. I don't know what this is about, but you'll get no bother from me, man. If you want money or whatever… just let me know. I'm sure we can work something out.'

He looks back, only eyes in a balaclava, turns away. Kills the light and locks the door behind him.

That's it?

He didn't hurt me but didn't give me any news. I don't know anything more than I did before, which was fuck all to start with.

I groan, shift back from the wall, stretch out a bit. He couldn't have given me a blanket or something?

Idiot. He took your clothes. He wants you to suffer.

The speakers scream, make me jump, jerk my ankle against the cuff and the pain flares up again. They keep on screaming, that awful distortion going right to my stomach and louder now. Constant.

And of course it's not an accident. This is his play. Chained up like a dog and now this near-deafening distortion going on and on.

He wants me to suffer. He doesn't want me to sleep. Doesn't want me to think straight. With the noise, there's no space for much else.

How am I supposed to find my mind in all this?

I plug my fingers in my ear canals, but there's no escaping it.

Just a test, remember. A game.

Some sick fucking game.

God, I feel it in my head. But surely that's just in my

mind. Psychosomatic.

It doesn't matter. It's still just an appearance in consciousness. An appearance that won't go away.

How's that for impermanence?

The distortion laughing at me.

Might never stop. I could die with this horrible noise still in my ears.

Sooner rather than later.

I can't stand it. My stomach moans louder. Feel sick. He's not going to stop it. It'll go on forever.

Never mind forever, just think about now. Stay in the moment.

But I feel it in my body where I can't control. In my head. Jesus, I am gonna be sick. Where can I go? Quickly. Not here. In the corner.

I crawl as far as the cuff will allow. Mind the piss. Vomit burns my throat, splatters the wall and floor. The speakers scream on and on. A second blast. Burning. Scratching. But then it feels a bit better maybe, if it weren't for the noise.

I shuffle back and awkward-lean against the wall. My throat's so dry. Head aching too. I need some water, but there's nothing here.

If he knew how shitty this felt, would he still do it?

What do you think? He gets off on this. He wants you to suffer.

For what? What did I ever do to him? He must be a fucking psycho, and the other one if he's still involved. The driver. There's no need for this. He's just fucking with me.

He's the antithesis of everything I learned on retreat. Trapped in identification with his sick ego. Grasping for whatever he wants and treating everything else with hateful aversion.

I could kill him if I needed to. If I were free and got the drop on him, I could do it. If necessary. Sometimes you have to use violence. To save your life.

Go on then. Do it.

He won't give me the opportunity. Can't do shit like this.

I kick at the cuff a few times again to test its strength. Maybe if I kicked hard enough a few hundred times, it would break. Would destroy my foot but maybe.

I shouldn't be here. I shouldn't have to do this. I left all of this behind. I changed.

Distortion screaming screaming screaming.

My ankle aching from the position.

Fuuuuuck.

I punch the wall. Twice. Three times. Again again again. I'll fucking kill him. If he doesn't kill me first. It's only gonna get worse. I won't let him do this to me.

Stop, Sam.

It isn't helping.

I lean my head back on the wall. Knuckles stinging. Blood starting to drip. Glowing hot. I keep pressing them to my lips to suck the blood away, but more drips onto my legs.

Fuck. Why did I do that to myself? Just make myself suffer more. And nothing to wipe the blood on. Just let it run until it clots. I feel the skin hanging off my middle knuckle and tear it off.

Fuck, man.

Calm. Be calm. Be with the breath.

Yes.

Inhale.

Exhale…

Inhale.

Can't even think with the damn noise. How am I supposed to be mindful? In the monastery it was easy. But here…

So don't be here.

In the darkness, the only spacial cues are the noise and the feel of the wall, the ground beneath me. Can't do anything about the noise. But I shuffle back from the wall, come to a meditation pose. Kiss my sore, bloody knuckles a last time, hold my hands in my lap.

I'm in the monastery. Not here. Sitting in the shrine

room with my eyes closed. Where I'd normally sit on the left by the wall. The PA's just malfunctioning. That's all the noise is.

Use it as a test. Let's see how mindful you really are.

I'm alone here. But in the shadow of him. A few feet ahead of me and a little to the right. Eyes half-closed, half-smile on his lips. Late afternoon sunlight kissing his shoulder. But his own light radiating out infinitely.

And me, a mindsick creature begging at his feet.

Never worthy. I'm just a psychotic ape to the enlightened.

And no escape from this reality.

You do it all to yourself. You know kamma.

And I'm supposed to tune this shit out with it blaring in my fucking ears every second? And just take it as any old sensation like the breath or an ache in the back? And that too, the aches and the exhaustion. No monk could stay mindful in this. The Buddha didn't get enlightened locked up in a dark basement with this fucking racket.

You have to try. What's the alternative?

Give up. Give up the fight.

And you'll suffer less that way? Not likely.

I try to visualise the room again, but it gets lost in the noise. Forget the room. Just be with the darkness. Darkness is better. The safety of ignorance.

Need to focus. Shut everything out that doesn't serve me. Slip through the noise and be here, where it's safe and nothing can really hurt you because there's no you to begin with.

Exhale.

Yeah. It's hitting now. Shouldn't have done it. I could have resisted but I was weak. Sneaking around in the cold and dark for a cigarette. What would the other bhikkhus say if they knew?

Just this once. It's okay. The stress has been really bad today. Just needed to calm myself for a minute.

It's just more grasping. A quick dopamine hit. Synthetic calm.

Yeah, but without it, I'd lose my mind. Got to keep my cool around Rich. He probably suspects something's not quite right already. Probably making up his mind right now about me. Judging me. And is he wrong?

Who cares what he thinks? As long as he doesn't catch me yelling out in my sleep or shaking like a junky. Let him think whatever he wants. I can sit as long as any of them. It's easy to detach from your mind when it's such a mess.

Is that true?

I stub out the end of the cigarette on the fence, go to toss it, but catch myself, push it into the box of cigarettes instead.

Retrace my steps in the darkness.

He's sitting at the table with a cup of tea, looks up from his book.

'Sam. Hello.'

'You alright?'

'I just made tea. You want some?'

'Erm. Yeah, okay. I'll take a little. Thanks.'

He pours me a cup and moves over so I can sit.

'You smoking?'

'Hm?'

'You were smoking a cigarette?'

'Oh, yeah. Just the one. I'd quit, but I don't know, I was weak today.'

'Mmm. These things are hard. Smoking worst of all. And very damaging for the mind. Everyone always talks about what it does to your lungs and your heart, but no one talks about what it does to your mind. But it can draw attention to the mechanics of the monkey mind. It took me years to quit. One of the hardest things I ever did. But that was out in the real world. Here, it's easier. Away from the distractions of the world. The conflict and the endless noise. How are you finding it here?'

'Yeah, it's nice. Peaceful. But I don't know, I think it'll

take me a little while to get used to it.'

'Mm. It's hard at first. For some people it's like a weight off their shoulders as soon as they get here. They just relax right away and fall into it. But for others it's hard. Out in the world, you're so conditioned to it. But eventually, the mind comes to rest. Once it loses its taste for worldly pleasures and excitement and always having the next thing and the next. You hold your own happiness hostage until you get something or achieve something or be something, but always moving the goalposts. Even in here it's easy to do. But it's better I think, being around other people on the path.'

'Mm. Definitely.

Is he always this philosophical?

'What's the story behind your tattoos?'

'Oh these?' He holds his hands out. What does it say? There's Dhamma. Buddha. Kamma. Sangha. Sati. Dukkha. A dozen words scattered across the back of each hand. 'When I started to get serious with Buddhism, in my twenties, about your age probably, I'd write the names of the triple gem on the back of my hand, Buddha, Dhamma, Sangha, to help me remember throughout the day, you know. But after a while, I got tired of re-writing it every few days, and made it permanent. And then I went back and added more.'

There's samadhi too. Nibbāna. Samsara. Anattā. Anicca. Moksha.

He surveys his hands too, as though he weren't so familiar with the tattoos himself.

'I like it. You've got all the main ones on there.'

He smiles, drinks his tea. Lets the silence linger. Only the slight electrical buzz of the light.

I drink my tea.

'What was your life like? Back in the world?'

He's not supposed to ask. You don't ask cons what they're in for.

'Alright. I mean it wasn't fulfilling me on a spiritual level, so I had to find something else. Somewhere else.'

'Mm.' He nods knowingly. 'Like most of us here. Apart from the few born into it. You have a lot of pain in you I see.'

What does he see? He doesn't know shit.

'Don't we all?'

He smiles. Waits.

'I lost a friend.'

'I'm sorry. It's always hard. Lots of dukkha. But pain can be a gift too.'

I'm about done with this. He means well, but I'm tired and I don't need to hear this.

'Yeah. It'll be fine though. I'm good. Thanks for the tea, man.'

He only nods, smiles as I retreat to my room.

'There you are.'

'Hey.'

'I was worried you'd gone.'

'Nah, I just came out to smoke.'

'Well great minds think alike.'

'Great addicts think alike.'

'Hey, speak for yourself. I'm just a social smoker.'

'Alright, yeah, fair enough.'

'Nah. I can't lie. I just smoke socially. And when I'm really stressed. Or depressed. Or when I'm with El… Okay, fine, you got me.'

'No judgement here.'

'Good.'

She leans on me while she digs in her bag for her cigarettes, puts one in her mouth. 'Goddamn it, where's my lighter? I'm so bad at keeping track of lighters honestly.'

'Here. Keep this one. I've got at least another one on me.'

'Aw, thanks man.' She lights, leans back against the wall, exhales. 'I'm having such a good time, though. This is some good shit. But not just that. I mean, everyone's really nice, and they were playing some absolute tunes.'

'Yeah, I saw you dancing.'

'Oh God. I'm sorry you had to witness that, but in my defence, you didn't need to watch.'

'It's true.'

'You much of a dancer yourself?'

'Ha. I mean I can two-step in the club. I have like five moves I rotate. But no, not really. I've never tried to specifically learn any moves.'

'Well me neither, man. I just like find the rhythm of the song and let it guide my body. Sometimes it works, sometimes not so much.'

'As long as you're having fun, who the fuck cares right?'

'Exactly.' Exhales. 'What kind of stuff you like? Music-wise I mean. You look like you've got a bit of a rocky vibe to you.'

'Oh yeah? I mean yeah I do like a little metal and I play the guitar when I can motivate myself, but mostly I listen to electronic and hiphop these days.'

'Oh nice. Like what kind of artists?'

'At the moment, I'm listening to a lot of Bonobo and Jon Hopkins. And Maribou State. They're like one of my favourites.'

'Yeah, man. Love Maribou State.'

'Oh really? What else you like?'

'Aw don't put me on the spot like that.'

'You asked first.'

'That's true…Shut up. I don't know, man. Just a bit of everything, you know.'

'That's not an answer.'

'Okay, fine. I don't know, a lot of pop music I guess. I got into Grimes lately. Childish Gambino. Um Kid Cudi. But like rock and R&B and some blues and jazz. *A bit of everything.*'

'Nah, touche. Sounds good to me.'

'Mm.' She closes her eyes, smiles. 'The breeze feels nice. It was so hot in there.'

The door opens. Ella comes out, lighting her cigarette even as she crosses the threshold. 'Hey girl.' She hugs Mina. 'How you guys doing?'

'Amazing.'

'Aw yeah. That's what I like to hear. I think Aaron wants us gone soon, but we can go back to mine? I don't want to end the night here - Hey, Sam, you got any ket?' Lowers her voice even though it's just the three of us.

'I do.'

'Cool. Yeah, afters at mine?'

Mina smiles. 'Sounds good to me.'

I pass the joint to Mina, exhale.

'Thanks. I probably shouldn't smoke too much tonight.'

Ella sits up. 'I thought we were all doing K?'

'Yeah, exactly, so I don't want to smoke too much, at least before. I don't have the tolerance you guys have.'

Ella takes the joint, hits it. 'Mine's not that bad. It used to be worse. Sam'll have the highest.'

Go in my bag for the right baggie. Yeah, that's the ket. Where's a plate? Or a mirror? I take a DVD at random from the bookshelf. *Bridget Jones's Diary*. Use my card to cut six vertical lines bisecting all their eyes. Snort the first line.

Mina leans over for a second look at the DVD box.

'Very nice.'

'That's about my level of artistic ability. I can also do a great permanent marker moustache. You can find my work in old magazines and school textbooks.'

She takes the box and rolled fiver.

'Should be in a gallery.'

'To be fair, some of the modern art I've seen, it wouldn't surprise me.'

'That's so true. But some modern art is really cool actually.' She does the line and pulls a face like she's maybe going to sneeze, passes Bridget Jones to Ella, who passes me the joint.

Round and round the circle.

'What's your favourite?'

'Art? Oh man, um, I really like Kandinsky. And the impressionists. Dali obviously, and a lot of surrealism. Van Gogh.' Pronounces it the Dutch way. 'He's one of my favourites. I mean, I know it's an obvious choice, but you know there's a reason most of the greats are so popular.'

As she talks, her voice drifts slowly away from me, and I have to pull myself back. Hit the joint. She wanted to play it safe. I leave the joint in the ash tray. If she wants it, she can take it. Ella hands Bridget over, wiping her nose with the heel of her hand, and reaches for her gin.

I do the line and wash it down with my beer.

Mina's just watching me, a half-smile on her face.

'You alright?'

'Yeah.' Laughs. 'I'm actually having a great night. Like I was having a bit of a shitty week, but this has been fun. I can't believe we haven't met before. Like you and Ella hang out quite a bit right?'

At uni and when she needs weed.

'Yeah, but we haven't been on that many nights out together.'

'Yeah, cause you're always busy,' Ella says.

'I know. I wasn't complaining.'

'Better not be.' She smiles, lights a cigarette.

Mina's turn. 'You want your second line now or later?'

'Oh, thanks.' She takes the box and snorts her second.

Really relaxed now. Working its way into my muscles like a warm bath. It's been a little while. The music filling the room, but where does the room really end? The music's distant, like a half-remembered dream, just the same as it's right here and now.

Could maybe hit the joint again. Yeah, fuck it. I hit it, and Mina keeps one eye on the joint, takes it when I offer.

'Oh, you reckon I can get a twenty-bag for the morning? My parents are away for the whole day, so I'll probably just get high and do some drawing.'

'Yeah, of course. Sounds nice.'

'Yeah - Dom accidentally took my weed when he was over last night,' she tells Ella.

'Where's he tonight then?'

'He was jamming with his band, then went out in Camden.'

'Oh, yeah, sorry, I did ask already.'

She's seeing someone. Never came up.

Well, that's that then. Getting ahead of myself like usual.

I finish my beer, hit the joint.

'I'm just gonna go toilet while I still can.'

'Aw, I already don't want to move.'

My body drags itself out the living room, unnaturally conscious rag doll. Up the stairs. In the bathroom, search my pockets for the ket. Another key per nostril. Check my face in the mirror.

Pupils wide. Hair messy, but I can fix it a bit. Stare into my eyes for a second until the world blurs and, for all I know, there's nothing else in existence.

Wish it would stop. Just for a moment so I can think straight. So I can remember what it was like without the fucking noise.

Head pulses. So uncomfortable, but what's the point in moving? Might relieve it for a second, but then it'll be right back to the same sensations somewhere else on my body.

It's just constant, overwhelming my senses. So tired, but I can't sleep. My body calling for it all the time, but something blocking it. Fucking noise.

And even with my fingers in my ears, it's still too loud and I can't stay in that position too long.

Can't sleep even though I know staying awake is doing more damage to my body and mind. Can't eat or drink either. Just burning up my energy here. Those older instincts tricked into keeping me alert to the noise. But it's okay. You can shut down. It's safe to sleep here. Just for a little while.

If only.

Notsafe notsafe notsafe.

My body needs to recover. Everything aching. Snivelling. And my head. Like a flu.

Just need it to stop. Just for a minute.

You deserve it. You piece of shit. You might fool the others, but you don't fool me. I know what you are.

Just want to get high. When I'm high, everything's okay. Then they can do whatever they want. But I haven't been high in years, and I don't have food or water let alone chemical comfort.

But still, behind the noise, implied by the noise, is silence. God, I just want a minute's silence. That's all I'm asking for here.

Sam.

He won't stop until I've lost my mind. I'll rot in the darkness. And even then he won't be happy. It won't do him any good.

Sam.

Inhale.

Don't get lost again. Stay with it.

What's the point? I'll just get lost again the next moment and down here it's so fucking hard to find it again.

This is what you trained for.

You thought it was gonna be easy? Maybe you're fucked after all.

You haven't died before. It's not gonna be pleasant. Especially not that way.

That's kamma.

Fuck this.

Push myself up. Sit as straight as I can, a puppet's string threaded through my spine pulled taut. Close my eyes again.

Watch the breath. That's easy. Don't worry about the rest. Just stay here with it.

Inhale.

Exhale. The lungs and the solar plexus. The air inside my nostrils.

And again.

Forget the noise.

Just the breath.

It'll be okay.

How can you say that? I'm going to die a slow, painful death down here. If he doesn't kill me violently. Wish he would. At least it'd be quick. Better than living like this.

Inhale.

God, I just wish he would stop screaming. Then things would be alright. Better.

Exhale.

Inhale…. Ex-

It stops.

Oh Jesus, it actually stopped. Ears still ringing with it, screws driving in. I shiver and nurse my ear canal with a finger.

Footstep on the stairs.

He's coming. Is he?

Yes. Another. Outside now.

Right?

Unless you're imagining it. Is it just sleep coming on? Am I finally falling asleep?

Sshhh. Stay here. Don't think about it.

The door opens. Light snaps on.

Squint. The more I open my eyes, the more it stings. Still stinging but not quite as bad.

He closes the door, steps in. Hammer. He's holding a hammer. Drags the chair over to the middle of the room, wooden feet scraping on tile.

No balaclava now. Just a normal-looking fifty-something man. Aside from the manic glare. Unnatural clarity. Doesn't look like he's slept much either.

Sits in the chair a few feet away. Lights a cigarette. Sniffs, glances over to the corner, and turns his nose up, glances at me with a look of disgust.

And that's my fault? I had to. You didn't give me any other choice.

Smokes his cigarette. Turns his lighter over and over with his free hand. Says nothing.

I clear my sore throat. 'Hey, listen man, I've got money. A few grand in cash. More in the bank. Let me go and I'll give you every penny. I won't say a word of this to anyone. On my life.'

'Shut the fuck up. I don't want your dirty money.'

'What do you -'

'Shut up!' I flinch from the anticipated strike but he only stares at me. Smirks. Sucks on his cigarette. Stubs it out and lights another. Not looking at me, just staring at the wall over my shoulder. Knowing he has all the power.

Then he looks into my eyes, keeps looking after I've averted mine.

'You know who I am?'

Does he want me to answer? Or is it rhetorical?

'No. I don't know you, mate.'

'Mm.' Raises his eyebrows, looks like he's on the edge of tears or another paroxysm. Then flicks the second cigarette into the corner, gets up, and makes for the exit.

'Please. Can I just have some water? Just a cup.'

He hears me but doesn't respond. Leaves the light on.

Just me and the basement again. The shelves of tools and nondescript boxes. Surely a bunch of things I could use to break this cuff. If I could just get to them.

Can maybe reach the chair. I shuffle as far out as I can and extend my other foot to hook the chair leg, draw it a couple of inches closer.

Footsteps on the stairs again.

I sit back as he returns, nursing a laptop and charger under his arm. He eyes the chair and then me suspiciously, drags it back well out of my reach, sets the laptop down, plugs it into the wall by the door, then opens a file. A video - fullscreen now - mother with a baby.

He walks off, hesitates in the doorway, then snaps off the light and slams the door.

Just the video now.

The baby's passed to an older woman. Looks suspiciously at her, back at Mum.

'It's okay, honey. It's just Nana.'

Rubs her little hand.

The baby smiles, but when Nana tries to hug her properly, she screws her face up and starts crying.

'I better take her back. She'll get used to other people soon. It's okay, love. It's okay.' Rubbing her back. Everyone smiling, watching this new life with awe.

Cut - adults stood around talking. The camera finds her. Sitting in her high chair with a Peppa Pig bib around her neck.

Happy birthday to you. Everyone singing. The bodies part and he comes in, carrying the cake with the single flickering candle.

Happy birthday to you.

He holds it in front of her chair. She reaches for the cake, but it's too far.

Happy birthday, dear Mina.

Happy birthday to you.

'Are you gonna try and blow it out, love? Look.' Mum mimes blowing out the candle.

She tries to blow-spit at the candle, but after a few failed attempts, Mum blows the candle out.

'Well done, honey.'

Everyone clapping and cheering and Mina initially surprised, then beaming.

Dad cuts a small slice and sets it down on Mina's tray. Mum tries to feed her a spoonful, but Mina grabs a messy handful and mostly gets it in her mouth.

A few people laughing.

Cut - still the party. Mina totally engrossed in a new plush rabbit, Dad stuffing a bin bag with wrapping paper. People chatting in the background. TV on. Some Disney character talking.

Mina tries to put the rabbit's face in her mouth, but a gentle hand deters her.

'Is that your favourite, honey?'

Mina stares up. Babbles something.

'What about your lovely dress? Can you say thank you, Nana?'

Mina looks around, babbles again.

'I'm sure that's her way of saying thank you.'

'Bless her, I think she's just a bit shy. She's usually quite a chatterbox.'

A song starts up, and Mina looks up to watch the TV. *The Jungle Book.*

Cut - a little older now, three or four, with sunglasses, sitting on the grass with other kids and parents. Music and talking, a girl screaming. Mum eating a hot dog. 'We'll need to put some more sun cream on her. It'll be wearing off by now.'

'*We* need to?'

'Fine. You need to.'

'Mm. Let the record show.'

'Shut it, you.' She reaches over to touch where he must be.

'Mummy, where Ella?'

'I don't know, love. Probably gone to get some food. We'll have to go look for them in a minute.'

She gets up and looks around.

'Not now, honey. In a few minutes. Let Mummy finish eating first.'

Okay, enough.

I get it. I don't need to watch this. It's what he wants.

Curl up facing the wall. Close my eyes.

Look for the bare necessities.

The simple bare necessities.

Forget about your worries and your strife.

Aw, she loves this one.

It's her favourite. Must have seen it a hundred times by now.

Plug my ears with my fingers.

Now just my blood pumping through my head. And the voices. But muffled. In another room.

It's okay like this. If I can't hear them, it's not so bad.

They loved her. She probably loved them too. And now she's gone.

I always liked animals. Since I was a little girl.

We've known each other like forever.

So fucking tired. Just let me sleep. It'll be okay if I can just sleep.

Who am I?

The melody. Not Jungle Book. The other one. What is it?

Is it on the film or just in my mind?

I draw one finger out of my ear.

It is the film. Kids singing. In a hall. A school performance or something. I know the song. God, what is it?

Can't remember. Some old pop song. Who cares?

Just try and sleep. Plug my ear again. My left hand aches against the floor. But sleep's more important.

Please.

Exhale.

Inhale.

Exhale.

Let me rest for a minute at least. Calm my mind.

You deserve this. You piece of shit. If she hadn't met you, she'd still be alive.

And I haven't suffered enough for it?

You think a few years meditating saves you from your kamma?

You're gonna fucking die down here. You'll die before your eyes see daylight again.

I hope he makes it hurt. I hope he drags it out for years.

I light another cigarette, skip the song. That's better.

A dad with his wife and young daughter gives me a wary look but I ignore him.

Not much further now.

I'll hang around for a few minutes, then get the tube and meet Conor. Only a couple more drops to make, and then if no one else makes an order, I'll head home. Smoke myself. Maybe play some Xbox. Should really study, but I can do that tomorrow.

She should be up here. By the bandstand, she said. But it's only an old couple on the benches.

There. Sitting to the right of the stand looking down at her sketchbook.

I cross the grass to her, and she looks up.

'Oh, hey. That was quick.'

'I was already out. What you drawing?'

She instinctively hides the sketchbook against her chest when I lean over but then shows me.

It's the bandstand, but she's added a couple of small fairies, one floating by the far post, one perched on the roof. A couple in masquerade masks and formal dress inside the bandstand, her clutching his outstretched arm. His mask half-black and half-white split down the middle. Hers patterned like a jigsaw.

Just in pencil, greyscale, but so detailed. She's even captured the lighting in the shaded shadows.

'That's amazing. Wow, I really like it.'

'It's not finished yet. And I'm thinking of adding colour. I might do it when I get back, but I've got this oil piece I've been working on all week I need to finish. I don't know.'

'What's the other piece?'

'Oh, I don't really know how to describe it. It's just like trippy patterns with plants and insects and shit.'

'Damn. I'll keep an eye on your Instagram.'

'Yeah. Well, I'll only put it up if it turns out well. Otherwise, I might just keep the picture for myself and paint over it because canvas is not cheap let me tell you.'

'Well it sounds very cool.'

'Thanks.'

I go in my bag for her three-five, hand it over.

'Oh, cheers. One sec.' She checks her cardigan pockets, then her bag, finds her cash. 'You want to smoke for a minute while you're here?'

'Sure. I'm in no rush.' There's no cops around. Pretty secluded.

'Cool. You might have to roll for me though. I'm not great under the best of conditions but outside with the breeze, I can't promise a pretty joint.'

'It's fine. I can roll.'

She has papers and roaches but no grinder, so I just break bits off the bud and crumble it with my fingers.

Spark the joint and get it going.

'What made you think of fairies and masquerade?'

'I don't know. I was just daydreaming I guess. It looked too lonely as it is. You know, it's the focal point of this area. It's designed for people to play music and dance and huddle out of the rain, but most of the time it's just empty. I don't know, it needed some livening up.'

'Yeah, well you certainly did that.'

'Thanks.' She hits the joint and exhales into the sky. Closes her eyes to savour the first rush. She looks so serene. Pretty. But don't. It's not worth it.

She hits it again and passes it back.

'How was your comedown after Saturday night?' I ask.

'It actually wasn't that bad. I mean don't get me wrong, the Sunday was a complete write-off. I just lay in bed the whole day smoking and watching Netflix. And I wasn't sharp even on the Monday. Work was a bit of a drag, but I've had worse. Definitely worth it. It was a good night. I had a really nice time.'

'Yeah, me too.'

'We should do something again soon.'

'Yeah. I mean I'm busy this weekend, and maybe next as well, but sometime it'd be nice.'

'Yeah, definitely. Well let me know when.'

She passes the joint back, exhales, stares off into the swaying trees.

'You ever think like reality's not real?'

'What do you mean?'

'Like the world that we experience through our senses,

that we see, hear, touch.' She brushes the grass with her fingertips. 'We never experience the world directly. We only experience the version of reality our senses create. You know like is my blue the same as your blue? Is your reality the same as mine? Or the same as a bird's or a dog's?'

'I mean there are similarities of course, universalities, but it's all subjective at bottom right?'

'Exactly. Like there are frequencies other animals hear that we can't. Colours they can't see. But they don't know what they're missing. You can't explain colour to a blind person. There must be so much energy out there, but we just interpret this narrow little bandwidth of it, and we call it reality, like it's something objective and ultimate. Sorry, I'm talking shit again. Ignore me.'

'No, I'm with you. I mean I've been aware of that kind of thing on psychedelics. And from what I've read, that's what a lot of psychology supports. But people don't like to think in that way.'

'No. They get so tied up in their little lives that they forget the big picture. That we're just insignificant lifeforms on a speck of dust hurtling through space.'

'But our lives can still have meaning.'

'Oh, sure. Like our lives have as much meaning as we want to give them. Some people just want to consume and hoard wealth and fuck and have babies and try to avoid thinking about their own mortality. And I'm not criticising. Maybe we're just wired for that life and for most of us there's no point fighting it, but that's just not me.'

'So what do you want?'

'Me? I don't know. I just want to do my art and hopefully bring some love and beauty into this world. And if I meet the right man and we have children, then I'll teach them to do the same. But I won't live like my existence is defined by marriage or children or a career. At the end of the day, I just want to live free and be happy.'

'Mmm, sounds good to me. I like that you know what you want. Not many people have that.'

'What about you? What do you want?'

'I don't know. Yeah, I want to be happy obviously. I want a meaningful job that isn't some corporate bullshit, just making money for some rich fuckers. Ideally something that'll help people. Probably psychology-related. And do some creative stuff on the side. Maybe record some music.'

'Nice. Yeah, I'd go crazy if I didn't have my art. It just takes me to another world where none of this matters.'

'Mm. You ever done psychedelics?'

'I mean, I've done mushrooms a couple of times but it wasn't too strong. I want to try acid sometime.'

'Yeah, it's awesome. If you have the right attitude with it.'

'Do you have some?'

'Yeah, of course. Not on me. But I can get you some next time.'

'Cool. Yeah, we should trip together sometime. I feel like I'd feel safe around you, and you obviously know what you're doing.'

'Well yeah, to be honest if anyone knows about drugs, it's me. But it's all about your mindset and the environment. If you're around cool people in a familiar environment and take a reasonable dose, not a lot can go wrong.'

'Hold on, we need a picture with El first.'

Even with my eyes closed I see the scene. Girls standing in front of the tree, all made up in their prom dresses. Mina hurrying off-screen.

Mutters and giggles.

'But after these pictures, we really should get going.'

And then cut to the girls climbing into the limo at the end of the drive, Mina last.

'Have a wonderful night, girls.'

'Watch your drink.'

The limo's engine changes pitch and it starts to pull away. The girls scream with excitement as they go, and the parents cheer and clap from the drive.

For the fiftieth fucking time.

Always leaving but never coming back.

I roll over and plug my ears, look for my breath in the chaos of pains and aches and discomfort across my body. My left side eases a little but the pain migrates to my right side.

You deserve it.

You'll never be comfortable again. Never free from pain.

Can't even sleep. Can't detach from these thoughts and feelings here. Where's madness when you need it? To draw me down, deep into my mind and away from all this shit? Some endogenous ketamine or psychedelic to shield me from reality.

Take it all away.

Mindfulness doesn't work. The Buddhists don't tell the whole story. Nothing can save you from this.

I'd rather die. Nothingness is better.

But still the fucking video. Even with my fingers in my ears, I hear her voice. And his. And her mother's. Her friends.

Just like he wants it.

They're all victims.

Breath. Don't forget the breath. They're just thoughts. Watch them.

I know.

Inhale. Exhale.

But it's so hard.

I know.

Inhale.

Footsteps. Outside the door.

Him.

Familiar click of the lock and creak of the handle. He steps in, snaps on the light. I'm ready for it, but it still stuns me. The ringing becomes pulsing in my head becomes nausea.

He throws something. I duck and it hits the wall behind me, bounces onto the floor. A water bottle.

Then the light's out and he's gone again. I scramble forward, half-forgetting the chain, and it scrapes at my already raw ankle. I grab the bottle, twist the cap off, and drink.

The water's cool, caressing my sore throat from the inside, and every drained cell of my body rejoices. More more more.

No. Stop. Don't drink it all now. You don't know when you'll get more.

Just a bit more. Half. Or thereabouts. That's enough now. Okay, just one more mouthful.

Save the rest for later. Don't want to risk being sick and losing all the fluid again.

The room fuzzes a bit while Mina and her primary school class sing. My head aches but a deeper ache now, in my brain, but you're not supposed to feel anything in the brain. There aren't pain receptors.

That can't be right.

Need to lie down. It's okay, just rest.

Just wish they'd stop fucking singing. And then I could rest for a minute.

And then and then and then.

You just don't want to be happy, do you? Always looking at the bad side. Thinking like one of them again.

The singing's quieter for this bit. The kids who can't remember the lyrics dropping off and the rest self-consciously mumbling. Just the piano across the hall keeping tune.

Have to make peace with it, I know. That or suffer. I've made peace with it a dozen times, but it just keeps playing and playing and there's no escape from it and I can't help but suffer from it.

Even if I can deal with the videos, there's no escape from the pain and the fucking insomnia. No one can stay zen under these conditions. Even a Buddha.

Round and round and round. Heard of samsara? Haven't we been here before?

It'll end one day. When I die. But how many more school plays do I have to suffer in the meantime? How many pre-prom parties and summer holidays and birthdays?

No more.

Soon you'll have a death date too. No death certificate. No one will ever know it, except maybe him.

Just mysteries.

Mum will never know. At best, she'll tell herself I disappeared to be a hermit in some distant monastery. But she knows I'd never go without telling her. Will she come looking for me? Maybe someone saw something. CCTV footage from the street they jumped me.

They'll never find you.

You'll never get to see her again. None of them. You forfeited that chance.

She'll live the rest of her life, knowing deep down something was wrong with you. Hoping, praying on her own deathbed that you're still alive out there somewhere.

I'm sorry. I tried to do right. I wasn't a bad kid. I just made some silly mistakes. You know I'm not a bad person.

Mina singing again with the guitar. Is it worse when she's older? Shades of the Mina I knew. But she's so pure when she's young. Innocent.

After a few more clips it'll loop again.

Maybe I should keep count to maintain my sanity. Yeah, like a tally of days scratched on a cell wall. It won't work.

You're getting caught up again. Stop thinking so much.

I'm just exhausted. Maybe if I block my ears and curl into a ball, I can sleep. Just for a few minutes at least. That's all I'm asking. Let me forget this room if only for a moment.

Need to piss. Don't want to get up yet, but the piss won't wait. Forget the robes. Just a t-shirt for now. That's fine.

The door handle won't turn. I try again, but it won't budge. It's locked. From the outside.

What the fuck?

Try again. Hard. No luck.

'Hey.' I hammer on the door. 'Rich... Rich, I'm locked in.'

Need to piss. Like now.

Try the door again. That's useless. You know that doesn't work.

'Rich.'

Can't climb out the window. I won't fit. Have to piss in here.

'It's for your own good.'

'Rich. Come on, open the door man, I'm about to piss myself.'

'You're going to have to get used to those walls.'

'Rich, open the fucking door.' Kick it once, twice, but it doesn't budge and now my ankle hurts.

Can't wait any longer. Have to piss out the window or in a bottle. Yes, here. Pour the murky water and cigarette butts out the window, push my glans into the bottle and piss. Keeps filling. The plastic turns warm in my hand. Getting kind of heavy now. Still pissing, the stream ricocheting off the inside of the bottle. Getting full now. Must be nearly done. But it keeps going and fills the bottle. I stop pissing only after the last of it splashes the floor and my robes.

What the fuck's this guy's problem? I should batter the door down and pour this piss down his throat.

'Fuck you, man. What gives you the right?'

'This is your kamma.'

I pour the piss out the little window.

I don't deserve this shit. Where's the justification? This isn't the way. This isn't the dhamma.

'Rich, you better let me out of here right now or I'm gonna break the fucking door down and beat the shit out of you. And then I'm gonna go to the abbot and get us both kicked out of here. You don't want that, do you Rich?'

He's gone. Or at least he's done responding to me.

Fucking prick.

For my own good. He doesn't know what's good for me. He's just trying to make me suffer. Sadistic bastard.

Like hurting me will make him feel any better.

I'll kill him if he have to. If I get the chance. I'll be ready.

My head swims, vision fuzzes.

God, not again. I need to sit down.

The room shakes, like the ground's moving under the building. Find the bunk and lie on my side. Whole room spinning and nausea gearing up.

Just want it to stop. Might never stop.

Need to piss.

I just went.

No. You didn't.

Still haven't finished the water. Should stretch it out a while longer. But then I'll have to piss in the corner again and smell it, and God forbid, I get critically dehydrated, I might need the fluid.

Can't wait much longer. Fuck it.

I probe along the wall for the bottle, down the rest of the water. God, that feels good. Like God itself in these meagre drops.

Head throbs.

'Watch your drink.'

Car engine starting up.

I kneel-walk towards the corner, push my dick into the bottle and wait to piss.

Come on, you need to go. It's only you here.

Watch your drink.

He doesn't say that twice, does he? Maybe he does.

I piss as much as I can. Wasn't much liquid in me anyway. Screw the cap on the bottle and leave it in the corner.

For later.

It won't come to that. He gave me this one.

It's not enough.

No.

My dick hangs between my legs as I crawl back.

Unseen mouths in the darkness waiting to bite.

Back to the hard, dirty floor. The familiar tiles still warm from my body. Absorbing my life. My tomb.

Baby's babble.

'It's okay, honey. It's just Nana.'

Then crying. Crying. Grating on my ears. I plug my right ear to mute the sound.

'I better take her back. She'll get used to other people soon. It's okay, love. It's okay.'

Babbles again.

Happy birthday to you.

Happy birthday to you.

Happy birthday to you.

Happy birthday to you.

Happy birthday to you.

Plug my other ear, but now my wrist aches. Try to take the weight off it but my core strength is shot.

Fuck.

Fuck this shit.

I can't sleep cause of the videos and they're so fucking loud. I'm losing my mind without sleep.

I can't reach the laptop, but there's the bottle now. The bottle.

I shuffle along and fumble for it in the corner.

Happy birthday, dear Mina.

Got it.

Happy birthday to you.

Back to the spot, on my knees.

Happy birthday to you.

Happy -

'Fuck you.' I hurl the bottle at the laptop as hard as I can manage, hit the screen, knock it back. The screen's cracked and tilted up but the video keeps going.

Fuck's sake. No. Let me try again. But the bottle bounced off in the right corner. I can't reach it, even with my leg.

Fuck man. Wasted the shot and now I don't even have the bottle in case I do need to drink it.

He won't be pleased.

What does he expect me to do?

A noise on the stairs?

Was it?

Wait and wait but he doesn't come in. Maybe he heard the sound. Maybe he's stood there listening in the dark.

I just want to sleep. Let my body rest a bit. And my mind. I'm just lying here but on constant high alert. He knows what he's doing. Sick fuck. My whole body aching. Feels like the ground's trembling. A constant low-magnitude earthquake. Christ, I am shaking. My legs the worst.

Need to calm down.

Watch the breath. You're lost in thought again. How long were you lost?

Inhale.

Exhale.

If not sleep, just rest.

You're only killing yourself here.

Probably for the best.

Inhale.

It's not going to be pleasant.

Exhale.

Don't want to be here. Let my mind wander. Visualise something. The monastery. No. Back home. In my room. But she's there too. And then we're in the park, at Ella's, trying to lose her but I don't want to lose her.

Her knowing smile. Like none of it matters.

You know it doesn't.

Flame flickers in the breeze as I light the joint.

Her eyes closed but rolling like REM sleep. Tracking private patterns.

Don't want to disturb her. Unless she's seeing something unpleasant. Then redirecting her might be a good idea. Best she doesn't have any more weed too.

But she opens her eyes, catches me looking. Smiles.

'What?'

'Sorry. I was just wondering if you were okay.'

'Yeah, man. I'm having a great time. This shit's fucking crazy.'

'What are you seeing?'

'Um, hard to describe, like this ancient architecture made of light, going on forever, and some faces popping up here and there, but like nice ones, you know, like they're a part of me. I don't know. It's more intense with my eyes closed.'

'Yeah, the closed-eye visuals are great.'

'What do you see?'

I close my eyes.

'Just patterns. Kind of kaleidoscopic.'

When I open my eyes again, Mina's skin flows, loosens on her face, like I'm watching her age in timelapse, but her features flow like ripples, never taking definitive form. Yet still a radiant beauty that isn't restricted to single lifetimes.

'You want to go for a cigarette?'

'Sure. I got this joint anyway.'

'Alright, cool. El, you want to come for a smoke?'

'I'm good here actually.' Looks back to the polar bears, slowly climbing the snowy incline. 'This looks so cool when you're tripping.'

'Yeah. Alright, back in a minute, love.'

She takes her cigarettes and leads us out the back. The world tunnels in the narrow hallway. Constricts us. Then she peels the door open, bathing us in the afternoon sun, and echoes of the door opening ripple through my mind. Dozens of versions of her opening dozens of doors.

Jesus, the weed's intensifying the visuals.

I go out after Mina, wave my arm in front of me. A dozen Shiva-hands trail after it.

Yeah, this is a good dose.

The garden's different from the other times we've smoked out here. More alive. Everything flowing. The garden drinking the sunlight and glowing with its energy, spilling out into the air, colours running and blending like paint in water.

Mina kicks off her shoes, descends the patio steps and crosses the lawn, spins around so her dress skirt floats about her waist. Stops.

'You coming?'

I follow her down, relight my joint and take a seat on the grass.

A speeding car engine in a nearby street. Birds twittering.

Mina lights her cigarette and hits it, trailing her fingertips through the grass.

'Having fun?'

'Yeah, man. You should try it. It's like you can feel the moisture inside the blades of grass.'

She takes my wrist and guides it to the grass.

'You're right. It's pretty nice.' The air in between the blades as much as the grass itself. Interdependent. The moisture and warmth slowly diffusing into my skin.

The world was made to flow. Things were never meant to be segregated and divided into little pieces. Only people do that. With our stupid intellectual minds.

Mina exhales and the smoke makes for the clouds, dissolves in the sunlight.

The weed's hitting me now. Feel it in my head, but it refines the imagery too. The tree bark shifts in timelapse, like stop-motion or flip book animation. Every ridge and wrinkle independent, knots expanding and shrinking, branches growing and sprouting leaves but somehow always remaining the same size and shape.

Mina's watching it too.

'How old do you reckon he is?'

'He? What makes you think it's a dude?'

'Look at him. He's a wise old grandad-tree. Almost looks like he has a beard.'

'Okay, yeah. I see it. I don't know. Maybe like fifty, sixty. But in tree years, that's probably like eighty. He's getting on.'

'He's seen some shit.'

'But he's still here, still keeping on.'

She eyes my joint. I offer it, and she hits it in between

her cigarette. Closes her eyes. Exhales. Ecstasy in her face.

Just breathe.

I close my eyes, and the fractals draw me in, some promise of home, of pre-natal bliss.

She hums under her breath. Some childhood rhyme.

Fucking hate the song.

Noise from beyond.

Was it just in the video?

Shit, was it?

He's on the stairs. Something hits the door low down. It opens, and he looks around, turns the light on.

I close one eye and visor my brow to see. Light still pierces my brain, threatening my stomach again.

He slams the door and glares at me. Jack Daniels bottle in his hand. Looks around again and spots the laptop and bottle of piss. Swigs his bottle, sets it slowly down on a shelf, then grabs the laptop, pulls it out of the wall, and throws it at me.

I jerk aside, but it still hits my shoulder.

'Fucking cunt.'

I press my hands to my new sore for all the good it does. But he's not done. He looks around, quickly settles for the chair, and hurls its full weight at me. I pull into a ball, most of it hits the wall, but it catches me in the knee. Pain that takes over everything else, everything but watching for his next move. Bracing.

He grabs the bottle of piss, drops to one knee, unscrews the bottle, grabs my jaw with one hand, I instinctively grab his wrist but I'm so weak I can't do anything anyway. He pours the piss, cold now, over my head, my face, clamping my jaw in place. I close my eyes, wait for it to finish, fucking stinks, hold your breath.

It hits my face hard, the weight of the remaining piss in the bottle.

He grabs my throat, but I didn't have time to breathe. Have to stare into his face, his insatiably angry eyes. Make it stop. Just for now at least. Please, just leave me alone.

'Who am I?'

Please. Going faint. I don't have the energy for this.

'Who the fuck am I?'

'Dad. You're her dad. But I didn't-'

He grips tighter, then releases me.

'I was her dad. Was. But now I'm your master. Now I'm your fucking God. And sadly for you, Sam, God's a fucking cunt.'

He kicks me, his hard shin bone in my stomach, side of my head.

He drags the chair well away from me, kicks the battered remains of the laptop at the shelves, turns out the light and closes the door.

Total darkness again, not even the glow of the laptop. Dead now.

I rest my head on the ground. The relative comfort of the dark lasts only seconds amidst the pain and nausea before the nightmares resurface. Can't see what's down here with me.

I jump at the speakers. Loud, so much louder than the laptop, black metal screaming now. Horribly distorted guitars and drums blasting at a thousand miles an hour. Distorted screaming. Growling. And then more on top. Must be a second layer, a second song played over the first. And a third? Feel it in my stomach, in my head. In my ears. So fucking loud. Wall of noise blasting me from the darkness. Even the ground vibrating from it.

And it's not gonna stop. It'll be more hours and more days of this fucking noise. Please. I can't do it.

No point begging now.

Shouldn't have thrown the bottle.

He'd have done it anyway. I couldn't stand the sound of it. But this is so much worse. No room for anything else, the horrible overlapping blasting.

Fucking bastard. I don't deserve this shit.

Need to calm down. It's too much energy. I'm burning

up. Just drop back. Come away from sensations and thoughts and feelings, away from these worldly phenomena and stay with awareness. Where it's safe. Where there's no suffering or grasping. Here, just a silent stillness.

And the tornado raging on out there.

But awareness itself holding all of it.

Breathe, Sam. Breathe through it.

But it's never going to stop. I can't take it.

Take what? These empty phenomena? And who is here to take anything in the first place?

Fucking idiot.

Please, I don't have the energy for this. Head's fucking ringing again. Maybe it's just the music. Can't escape it.

Multiple men screaming. Sounds never supposed to be played together. My mind wants to focus on just one thing, one instrument or melody, but just when I find it amidst the noise, another line pulls me away, then another. Churning me over and over.

Two of the songs pause for a moment, an unlikely beat of unison with only a third song playing, before the other two kick in, twisting off in opposite directions, wrenching me apart.

Nausea rolls through my stomach. It's sickening. Physically sickening. If there's anything but bile in my stomach to throw up.

Fuck you.

He knows exactly what he's doing.

Wake up, Sam.

You're in hell. You fucked up, and now he's got you chained up like his little plaything. And he's going to torture you until he gets tired of it, and then he's going to kill you. But that's a long way off.

He gave you the water.

I'll kill myself first. I won't give him the pleasure.

And how are you gonna do that?

Growling. They're here. In the darkness with me. Pressing in.

I shrink back, towards the pissy corner. Pulling on my sore ankle.

Eyes in the dark. Imagined? Low to the ground. Can't be human. Maybe a human flat on their stomach.

Gone now.

Losing my fucking mind.

No one's here.

You wouldn't have heard him over the speakers. While you had your eyes closed, he could have opened the door, let something into the room. A hungry dog. Or maybe he's here with me, waiting in the darkness.

No, please. I'm too tired to deal with this.

Try to be still. Don't let it get to you.

Something moves the hairs on my arm where it's not numb. Moves further down.

I slap it. Roll the remains in my fingers. Some bug. Spider probably. But now there are more in the darkness where it used to be safe. What else is out there, impeded by nothing but lack of a current motive?

Termites?

Rats?

So many eyes and hungry mouths.

Roll over.

God, it fucking stinks. The damp, earthy smell. Piss and sweat and sick.

Movement on my dick. Another insect.

I jerk to my back and wipe my dick. Careful. Feel around. Don't feel anything. Maybe I got it. Or did I just imagine it? Just a faint breeze? But there's no breeze down here.

Press my back to the wall, but what if things come down it? Maybe it's better further out.

Fuck, I'm losing my mind.

I face the room just in case. Got to be on guard. But the fucking sound hurts my head so badly.

Forget it. If someone's down here, you'll find out. Need to rest for a bit.

Lie down. Shut down. Preserve energy. Need food, but

there's none. No water left either.

Getting fainter. Probably a mercy. An escape from this. Let me out of my head for a bit.

Breathe.

One.

Inhale. Exhale.

Two.

Inhale. Exhale.

Three.

Inhale. Exhale.

Four.

What you up to tonight?

Well, I gotta make a couple drops. But after that, not much. Just chilling. Why?

Right, so you're coming to a house party is what you're up to. El didn't mention it?

Nah. Where is it?

Just in Greenwich. Some people were talking about going out after, but I don't know. We'll see. So you're coming?

Might know some people there. That could be a good or a bad thing. Can potentially push some shit too. What else am I gonna do? Sit around on my own and get high?

Yeah, alright.

Amazing. We're just drinking at El's now. Gonna head over at tenish.

I'll just have to meet you there then.

Okay, cool. And can you bring some Molly?

Yeah, will do.

I'll probably need some weed for the comedown too. A three-five?

Yeah yeah, I got you.

Alright. Cool. Thanks, Sam. Looking forward to seeing you.

Out of the tube station into the rain. Pull my hood up and

walk round the corner to the usual spot.

Not here yet.

Fuck's sake.

Light a cigarette and check my phone.

9:48.

Text from Ella: heyy heard ur coming tonight! Can u bring some charlie as well pls? Should be a good night!!

It's cute they think they need to remind me to bring drugs. In my bag and jacket, I've got pretty much everything. If I got searched by the feds, I'd be fucked. But I'll be fine. They probably wouldn't find the good stuff anyway. Just confiscate the weed and give me a slap on the wrist.

God, he's always late. If we didn't know each other so well, I'd just drop him. Don't have time to wait around, risking my neck for other people.

The girls will probably be a few drinks in by now. I'll be fashionably late to the party. It probably won't get properly going until at least half-ten. If it's that kind of party, which it sounds like it'll be.

Toss my cigarette away. Go on my phone so I don't look suss just standing here. Reply to Ella.

There he is.

'Hey, what's good man?'

'Alright bro?'

We walk down the road and make the exchange.

'Safe, man.'

'Have a good night bro.'

Anxious walking up to the high-rise. It's fine. What are you fucking stressing about?

It's holding all this shit. Being in some half-dodgy ends. People I don't know.

I text Mina to say I'm outside. How do I get in?

Want another cigarette, but I should save it so I can smoke when I get there if I need to. Is there a balcony? Or do I need to come back out to smoke? Maybe we can just smoke out the window.

Mina: Buzz 45. Someone will let you in.

I buzz the flat and the door clicks open. Take the stairs up, sweating and half-out of breath by the fourth floor.

Rap music spills onto the landing and you can already smell weed. Unless that's just me. Could be.

I knock on the door but no one answers it. Probably can't hear. I bang again, and Mina opens the door.

'Heyy.' She hugs me. 'How you doing, man?'

'Yeah, good, you? Party looks like it's getting going.'

'Yeah, man. We're just in the kitchen.'

Guides me through - she smells good - to the kitchen. El, Cat, some other girl, and the boyfriend. Dom, was it? Wasn't expecting him.

Well, that was your fuckup.

'Alright, Sam.'

'Hey.'

'You alright?'

'I had like five hours to write three thousand words.' Ella halfway through a story.

'Jesus, I've never had it that bad.'

'I drank so much coffee and Red Bull I was sick for like two days.'

'There space in the fridge?' I ask Mina, taking my beers out of my bag.

'Maybe, if you're good at Tetris. It was pretty full before.'

'Good luck, mate,' Dom says.

It's pretty packed, but I squeeze two in at the top, one in the drawer, crack open the fourth.

People talking in the hall. Laughing. The music sounds good. I should scope the place out, get some distance.

'Where do we smoke around here?' I ask.

'Good question,' Mina says. 'El... El, where we smoking?'

'I don't know, they were smoking weed in the lounge, but I don't know about cigs.'

'Whose place is it? Are they your friends?'

'Kind of. I'll go ask Mark.'

'Cool. I'll come with.'

Ella leads the way to the living room where most people are, a bunch seated around the coffee table, people standing by the window, by the TV. Weed smoke. Guy with his home decks and a Macbook. Thinks himself a DJ. Tunes aren't bad to be fair.

Ella waits for a pause in the conversation to address the guy. 'Hey, where do we smoke? Can we smoke up here or do we need to go out? Like cigarettes I mean.'

'Erm, if it's just one person at a time, out the window's fine, but more than that, you better go out front. We'll buzz you back in.'

'Alright, safe. This is Sam by the way. He's on my course.'

'You alright, mate?' We shake. 'Nice place you've got.'

'Cheers. Well it's my Dad's. He's away in New York for a week on business so I thought I'd get some folks over and make the most of the space.'

'Yeah, nice one.'

'Did you wanna smoke then?' Ella asks. 'I wouldn't mind getting some air to be fair.'

'Sure.'

Ella pokes her head round the kitchen door. 'We're just going out the front to smoke.'

'Ooh, I'll come,' Mina says. She and Dom follow Ella, and Cat trails behind.

'We're getting the lift though,' Ella says. 'Fuck the stairs in these heels.'

'Gotta get those leg gains in.'

'Go on then. You take the stairs.'

'Nah, fuck that. I just walked up.'

We have to wait for the lift to come up. A couple of guys get out with carrier bags and a crate of beer. Probably for our party.

Five of us squeeze into the lift. Breathing each other's sweat and fragrances. I drink my beer. Might roll a joint when we get back in. Talk to a couple of people. If they're smoking weed, they probably do other shit. But they might have shit in already. I'll put it out there for people who seem cool.

Door opens with an 8-bit chime. Ella kicks off a heel and blocks the front door with it, limps with her one shoe over to the wall and lights a cigarette. Dom gives Mina one who offers Cat the pack but she declines.

She's a good girl. I don't know what she's doing hanging around with us lot.

'So what we on tonight?' Ella asks. 'You got the stuff, Sam?'

'Of course.'

'What you guys fancy?'

Mina stares off, her face screwed up with thinking like it's a real conundrum. 'Molly's always good. I might just bomb it for now. Then we can always do bumps later. Can you sort that, Sam?'

'Yeah. You want the same, El?'

'Sure. Do me a 200 bomb? And another 100 for later.' In for a good night.

'You got a scale?'

'I think Mark does. I'll ask when we go back in.'

'Safe. Cat, I assume you're passing.'

'Um, yeah I probably should. Maybe later. We'll see.'

'Alright, cool. Dom?'

'I've got my own shit. Don't worry about me.'

'Alright.'

Upstairs, Ella gets the scale from Mark, and I take it into the bathroom to make the bombs. Swallow mine down with beer, and pass the others out. Give the scale back to Mark.

'Cheers for that, man. Anyone else on it tonight?'

'I think Josh and Tom are.'

'Well, I've got a little extra if anyone wants. Just let them know.'

'Alright, safe.'

Several conversations overlapping. Mina sitting with

Dom, his arm around her waist. Few new people. Ella chatting with Cat and Mina.

'They were cute though. Proper power couple. I think they would have gotten married if he'd lived.'

'Yeah, probably,' Mina says. 'But aren't all marriages doomed eventually? Celebrity ones especially.'

'Oh my God, stop trying to piss on my fairy tale.'

'I'm just saying. Look at the stats.'

Might roll a joint.

Sit against the wall, open a new twenty-bag and use my mini grinder. The new guys in front of the fireplace talk about some video game. Nothing I recognise. The girls I think they came with look cool. One's got too much of a grungy Amy Winehouse vibe, but alternative girls are generally fun.

One of the guys watches me roll for a moment. 'Smells good, man. What weed is that?'

'Hm. I think this one is northern lights. But I've got some lemon haze somewhere that's really good.'

'Ah nice. What's the one Jimmy Hendrix has a song about?'

'Purple haze.'

'Ah yeah, there's a few songs about that strain, aren't there?'

'I don't know. Probably.'

'And then there's the cheeses. Everyone loves a cheese. Yeah, northern lights is a classic too. But I prefer sativas myself. I like to be *high*-functioning when I smoke.'

'Yeah.'

I spark the joint and obviously he watches me smoke.

'You mind if I get a couple tokes off that, bro?'

Would have offered it anyway, but now part of me wants to say no.

'Sure. Pass it round.'

Got to escape the guy though.

Mina giggles. Lays her hand on Dom's leg.

Ella and Cat silent.

I pull out my phone and scroll mindlessly until the joint comes back. Only a half-joint now, there's so many people. Even Cat hit it. Maybe she's not as plain as I initially thought.

I don't have to stay too long. If it gets shitty, I can just slip out, make out like I have somewhere else to be. We'll see after the MD hits.

Wish there were more people I knew here. Could talk to those girls, but I need a good opening.

Meet Mina's eyes across the room. She rolls them. What's her problem? Is she stuck in dead-end chat as well or was she arguing with Dom?

At least I'm on it. God, that warmth all down my arms and legs. Dopamine flowing.

'Yeah, so I'll never vote Labour, even though I agree the Tories are completely out of touch.'

Mina makes a beeline for me. 'You wanna come for a smoke?'

'Sure - I'll catch you later, mate.'

She looks in the kitchen. People standing around talking and drinking.

'Shall we just share one out the window? I can't be arsed to walk downstairs.'

'Alright.'

She reconsiders. 'Actually fuck it, let's go down.'

'Alright. Thanks for rescuing me by the way. That guy was bringing me down.'

'Oh yeah? How's your high?'

'Yeah, good. Always a good time with this shit.'

'Yeah.' She strokes her top absentmindedly, runs her fingers down her arm. 'Thanks for sorting it. Let me know how much you want for it. Or I can just get you a couple of drinks when we're in town.'

'Don't worry about it. But I can sell you the weed and any downers you want for the morning.'

'Right, yeah, nice one.'

'What were you rolling your eyes at?'

'What? Oh, I don't know. Just how fake people can be. All the smalltalk and validation seeking.'

'Yeah, I was thinking the same. Everything alright with you and Dom?'

'Yeah. Basically. He just gets pissy when I take drugs. Even though he does more than me, he just doesn't like the idea of me getting high. He won't say anything, but he'll just be off with me the whole night. I can't be arsed with it.'

'That sucks.'

She blocks the door with her shoe and we light up. No one else here. Getting darker now.

Mina closes her eyes, her arms open to the breeze, a waiting hug.

'Mm. This is nice though.'

'Yeah.'

She stands closer to me. Leans in?

'You having a good night though?'

'Yeah, I mean hopefully it's just getting going, but I'm feeling good, man. No thanks to you.'

'Well, I have my supplier to thank. It's good shit.'

'Yeah.' She closes her eyes again, draws on her cigarette.

The door opens. Ella and Dom.

'There you are. I was looking everywhere for you, girl.'

'What, everywhere in the two or three rooms?'

'I thought you were in the bathroom for a while. Anyway, how's everyone doing?'

I light another cigarette.

Check my face in the mirror, then head back out.

That last key's really hitting. Need to watch my jaw. Should have brought some gum. The coke makes me want to talk, but Mina's busy with Dom in the corner. The girls must be in the kitchen.

They're not. Maybe they went out the front again. Or have they left? What time is it?

2:57. Jesus.

Text from Ella. They did leave. Goddammit. I'm on the up. I was ready to hit town. But looks like it's winding down here. Will anybody else be about?

In the living room, Dom and Mina are all cosy. Kissing.

Oh, fucking wonderful. And I'm supposed to talk to one of these cunts and try to ignore it?

Allow that shit.

I turn and leave the flat without talking to anyone. People will assume I left with the girls. I'll just go back to mine. Listen to some music. Smoke some weed. Or do some mushrooms. That'd be good. Get my trip on. And on top of this buzz, the visuals will be fucking crazy.

Forget Mina. Why do I even care? I'm just playing myself.

It's not far to walk. Yeah I'll smoke another joint and do some shrooms. Got those golden teachers saved.

I munch three-five of the teachers, wash them down with Coke. Gag but nothing comes up. Hate the taste, but can't be arsed to make tea. It's over now.

Hit the joint.

My head should be swimming after the amount of booze I've drank, but the coke overrides it. A clean slate. Like freshly settled snow. Haha. Snow.

But the coke will wear off soon.

Then it'll just be a drunk hippy flip. Plus the weed. Yeah, we'll see some crazy shit.

Should probably slow down. But it's too late now. And I deserve a good night. It'll be fine.

The mushrooms sit in my gut, soaking in the booze and stomach acid. Feel a bit sick. I've had nausea on shrooms comeups but not this bad. Just ride it out. It'll pass eventually.

Scroll mindlessly through YouTube but my mind goes blank and there's nothing interesting to watch.

It's getting worse. I might actually be sick.

I go to the bathroom and throw up in the toilet, half-digested mushrooms, beer, and the burger I inhaled for dinner.

Great, that means my trip won't be as strong. How much psilocybin did I manage to squeeze out of them? Could do some more. Or a little acid.

No that's crazy. Take the hint from my body to slow down.

Hope Mum didn't hear that. If she's back yet. Might still be out.

Back to the room. Feels better in here. Hug my arms around myself and sit back as the Molly radiates. The final wave of the coke buzzing in the background. Heart pumping. Lungs going.

Pleasure, and warmth, and numbness but somewhere amidst it all, an aching pain.

Don't think about that.

Should put some music on. Something trippy. Bicep will do.

Part of me is energised and doesn't want to sit still. Wants to move and dance and go somewhere. But another part is starting to melt into the chair. The show's just getting going.

But that pressure in my head. Like fists pressing against my temples and forehead. And still a hint of nausea. Or is it a fresh wave?

The music is quite fast and hectic. My body's restless, wants to move to the beat, but the more I move, the more uncomfortable and nauseous I feel, so I just lie back and close my eyes. But the weight of the experience and everything coming piles on. Flickering iridescent light.

It's better with eyes open. That way the visuals have to contend with the contents of the room. And I probably drank enough alcohol to make the room spin. Don't forget that. The coke starting to wear off now. Making way for the trip.

The room is starting to blur a little. Edges softening.

Surfaces melting. Faint waves in the carpet, the promise of deeper currents.

Maybe I absorbed a good dose of psilocybin before I threw up after all. And the weed and the Molly on top of it heightening it. Never done this particular cocktail before. Not with the coke. And so much booze. That's what gets you. If I stay off the ket, I'll be fine. As long as I don't check out and lose control of my body.

Head aches. Should drink some water. But I've already drank so much tonight. I was necking water with the girls. Gotta watch that shit. It'd probably only make me sick.

Something watching. Subhuman eyes watching always from the edge of my periphery but never in focus. The universe watching itself. But it can't know. Don't disturb it.

I probably won't go out with Mina again. Maybe the occasional night out, but she's a bit of a head-fuck to be around regularly. Probably has her own issues.

The music really grating now. Change it for something gentler. Bonobo. Always good for a trip.

Yeah, probably for the best. It was fun while it lasted, but let it rest.

Just back to the same loneliness, the same background ache. Maybe I'm not supposed to be with anyone.

Not good enough.

I wouldn't have the time for it anyway with the dealing. And uni and everything. Not many girls want to date a dealer. Not the good kinds anyway. But I wouldn't want to give up the money stream. It's about the one good, consistent thing in my life.

Until the feds are at the door and they fold you into the back of a squad car, ferry you to jail, and what use is all the paper then? They'll seize what they can find of it. Probably not the shit buried in the yard. But how many years of my life lost? And the things they'll do to you in prison. The places your mind will go.

I'm careful.

But they'll get you eventually. Your luck won't last

forever.

What do you need the money for anyway? Just fucking greed. That's it.

But it's not my fault we've been broke for most of my life. With piss-all from Dad, and only Mum's salary to pay for the house and the bills. It's nice to be able to help her out with the cash from participating in 'psychological studies'.

Starting to feel fuzzy. Warm inside but it's a little cold in the room. Hard to tell what's my actual physiology and what's my perception. The warmth is nice though. Like a wood fire glowing in a stove on a cold night.

But the nausea hangs around. Mingles with the headache.

The hangover will start to kick in before the comedown. Unless I keep drinking. Not a good idea. Gonna be a nasty comedown regardless.

The light stinging my eyes. Head singing like a bell. Singing singing singing. My body like a dead weight. Can barely move it without everything hurting.

Strange sensation on my skin. I scratch it away but it comes back on my arm.

Stomach really hurting. What's the problem? If you need to be sick, be sick. If not, shut up and leave me in peace.

The music's too melancholy now. Makes me feel like I could melt off the sides of the chair. An amorphous pile of clothes and jellied flesh.

That's not me.

Then who are you?

It's just the mushrooms kicking in. Everything blurring together. And the music. Could change it, but I don't have any energy left. It'll be over soon.

An echo of agreement. They're still watching. Always watching. You just forget. Should try to remember more. Always lost in my own mind.

Nice to get out of it for a while though. Yeah, just get out of my mind for a few hours. Before the gritty comedown. Forget the comedown. We'll just ride it out. Smoke some weed. Could hit a bowl now. Still on the comeup, but it might take the edge off the anxiety.

Could make it worse.

I sit up and grab my bong from under the desk, but only in my mind. The intention to move is fine, but the signal gets lost on its way to skeletal muscle. Shit, can't move anything. Paralysed. But I didn't take any ket, did I? We did the Molly and a little coke, I did some more on my own. Booze and weed. And the shrooms. I don't remember taking any ket. Unless we did at the party and I just forgot. It's possible. Jesus, I'm pretty fucked up right now. Maybe I mixed up a baggie and we did ket instead of Charlie or the MD.

Can't move to turn the music off now. Can't move to shift the aches and weird little sensations like insects on my skin. I'll just have to ride it out. As long as I don't vomit, I'll be fine.

But I do feel sick. Not quite like I need to vomit, but it could change in an instant. At least I'm kind of upright.

Really? Death within reach and that's your reaction? You're a sad fucking case, man.

And all for what?

Back aching. Sharp tingle of inaction.

If there was a fire or a burglar broke in, I couldn't move to escape. He could walk in right now, slap me around, throw me on the bed, rape my arse, cut my throat, and there's nothing I could do to stop him.

It's not fair. It wasn't my fault. I'm not a bad person. I just wanted to get fucked up. I wanted to feel good.

My eyes are so heavy they just want to close but when I let them, the eyes see me, with no reality to hide behind. They emerge in the patterns, ancient ethereal figures manifesting.

You're not real.

Melting into the chair now. Becoming the chair. Can't move my neck to see the far side of the room and the door.

What if Mum sees me like this? She won't understand. She'll call an ambulance when she can't get a response out of me, and they'll bring police. Find the drugs. They'll lock me up in a dark cell, alone in my mind and not even a toilet to shit in.

Like an animal.

The beat drones on and on, cranked up too loud on my laptop speakers. Distorts. Slows down, then speeds up. A grinding rollercoaster.

My body hums. Shaking by its own energy. But nothing I can do to move it. So tired. It thinks it's sleeping. It thinks I'm gone but I'm still here while the dream churns around me. In me.

Flickering light. Driving fast down a long tunnel. Vague sense of nostalgia. But I can't place it. Everything's fracturing, drifting away from each other before connections can form between them.

And what's left? Empty space? Blackness going on and on for lightyears and meeting nothing.

The carriage jostles dangerously on its tracks. The overworked engine humming like a mother trying to soothe her doomed children.

Rich smiles. Shakes his head.

Rich. I could use a little help man. You're a good guy.

He smiles again because he knows I know it's too late. We're on the wrong train.

You're really fucked this time, Sam.

I'm sorry. I had it all figured out. I don't know when it went wrong.

The light drains from the sky beyond. Something dying out there in the silence. No one deserves to die alone.

Crawling on all fours. Nothing I can do.

A noise through the wall. Or door. If something's already in the room with me, I'm helpless.

Come back. Sam, you need to come back.

Gonna be sick. Jesus, please, just take the pain away. I'll do anything if you just take the pain away.

It hits me in the back. I twist around, clutching for it, pulling at the cuff as his shadow slips out the door.

Blackness again. Still screaming and screaming.

What is it? I feel around with my arms and free leg, touch it, drag it back to me. A tin. With a ring pull. Get my finger under it and pull the tab up, like I've done a thousand times, but my fingers are so weak. The tab cuts into the flesh of my finger, need to try with my middle finger, get it open.

Smell it. Jesus. Cat food. The top flat and jellied. Got to be cat food.

My stomach kicks with disgust.

Sick bastard. Not even beans. Not human food.

You'll eat it though.

Not now. Fuck that.

You will. Soon.

Screaming and screaming over the drums and distortion.

Can't eat cat food. Like a fucking animal.

Like you have other options. It's that or death. And you don't want to die yet. Not really.

It's not right. I shouldn't be here. Pull hard at the cuff, jerk jerk jerk but it doesn't budge and only opens a new cut on my ankle. Wet and it stings when I touch it. The tiles must already be stained with my blood. And piss and sick and the rest of it. Seeping into the grout. My cells dying off and themselves becoming the room. Soon enough there'll be no me.

Heart beating away. Burning oxygen and glucose I don't have. Getting faint. Just lie still. Cross my arms and stroke themselves. Hold myself together. It's okay. I've got you.

 Shivering.

So weak. Need to sleep. But with the music and the stress of it all, there's no way. I don't know what's down here with me. Did he throw anything else?

Feel around with my leg as my head throbs. Just the tin.

He was angry about the laptop.

Shouldn't have thrown the bottle.

Can still smell the piss in my hair.

Maybe next time he'll bring water. If I'm good, maybe even proper food.

If I'm good.

I can't die down here. And there's no going out the easy way. He'll make you suffer.

Could I get through to him? Is there any humanity in him?

Feel sick. Just the smell of the cat food. And the noise. The endless screaming. Almost want him to come back just so it'll stop for a second.

How angry is he making himself out there? Getting himself all fired up, wasted and apoplectic until he grabs a knife out the drawer and comes to use it on me. Might not even see him coming.

I'd kill him.

You wouldn't stand a fucking chance.

Maybe he's calmed down a bit. Who knows what else he's doing out there. A job. Family. Mina never talked about any siblings but what about his wife? Is she up there? Does she know I'm here? Or is this some abandoned property no one knows about? Maybe they divorced. Grief can easily break the camel's back of relationships already on the rocks.

Maybe he has nothing to lose.

I should tell him about the suppliers. Blake's crew.

He won't listen.

But maybe I can get him to listen. It was one of them. Or their own plugs. I don't have an address but I have their number. And what are the chances of them using the same number three years later?

So I've got nothing.

But he found me.

How? Someone must have talked. Ella or Dom or someone. Someone spotted me. He must have been following me. Wouldn't have been hard to find me if he knew I was involved with the sangha. Aren't that many Buddhist centres in London. He'd know I lived in Greenwich.

What does it matter now? Doesn't matter who it was or how he did it. Just what he does next.

Stomach wails along with the cacophony. I have to eat the cat food. Just a bit. Don't have to eat all of it.

Save same for later.

Just a bit. Just to keep me going.

Reach for the tin along the wall, push two fingers into the jelly and break off a chunk, transfer it to my mouth, chew chew, chunks of meat embedded in the gelatinous fat. Old chicken or horse or something. The bits not good enough for human consumption. I gag. Manage to keep the food in my mouth, swallow. Come on. Chew chew swallow. Chew chew swallow. Pinching my nose to cut off the smell, push the tin away. Burp. Ready to turn and shuffle towards the corner to vomit. No water to wash it down. Lingering taste of the shit.

That'll do. I can't take any more. I'll be sick.

Just rest.

I place the tin by the wall and lean against the brickwork, but my ankle starts to cramp within seconds, so I lie down, my whole body buzzing, the floor vibrating like any second a hole might burst open and swallow me.

Fatty, slimy taste still on my tongue and the music-notmusic blaring. Something sounds almost brassy in it. A saxophone? Probably just imagining it.

The songs fighting each other like heads of a hydra. Snapping. Biting. Blood running.

It wasn't me. I don't deserve this.

This shit again?

They should be here in this hell. Blake or James or whoever the fuck it was. They're still out there, sitting tight and enjoying their blood money while I suffer for it.

You could have saved her.

Head burning. Exhausted but everything trembling. Legs worst of all. Straighten them out, pull them into my chest, but it makes no difference. Freezing down here. Mind churning like an engine. Need to stop thinking so much. Pull back. Where is awareness? Right here in all this. Awareness holding it together. Wish it would stop. Wish I'd die. I mean it. I want to die. It's too much. I can't be mindful here. What's the point anyway? Even if I'm aware the whole time, I'm still here. Still suffering.

Sam.

Easy for the Buddha to say, sitting on the soft ground under a nice Bodhi tree with the sun shining. He didn't have this screaming noise in his ears or the pain and endless aches or the insomnia or the taste of cat food in his throat.

He didn't sell drugs either or poison his mind for so many years. He didn't cling to sense pleasures and material shit. You brought this on yourself.

Sam.

Breath coming and going. In-out-in-out-in-out.

You're wasting energy. Energy you don't have. I don't have a choice. Better the life leaves me quicker. The sooner, the better. Before he can come back. Please, just take me.

That's not how it works. You don't get out that easy. There's a long way to go yet. He won't let you die. Not until you've suffered enough.

But it'll never be enough. It won't help him anyway. He's only torturing himself.

You're the one chained up in a basement.

Sam, for fuck's sake.

I have to try. If I give him Blake, maybe he'll let me go. Or at least I'd have another soul to keep me company down here.

Wouldn't hear him over the noise. Wouldn't see him in the darkness. Could be here now for all I know. Another mebutnotme to share in this suffering. He'd deserve it too.

I turn the corner and walk down the long road, the sounds of traffic growing fainter until I reach the spot. Lean against the wall, light a cigarette, and scroll Twitter to blend in. Keep it close to my chest to shield it from the rain.

Before I finish my fag, headlights swing round and stare

at me, getting bigger and bigger as the black Range accelerates, comes to a smooth stop in front of me.

I toss my cigarette and get in the back, bump Blake's waiting fist and James's. Smell of weed smoke and grime on the stereo. I feel the bass through the floor.

'Wagwan, bro? You good?'

'Yeah, man. You?'

'Yeah, yeah, calm.'

Blake pulls away and James goes in the glovebox and hands me a Sainsbury's bag. I check it's all there - four ounces of green, half of MD, half of coke, fifty pills but I won't count them now - then stuff it into my rucksack and hand him the cash. He counts it with the dexterity of a bank clerk, nods, folds it, and puts it away.

'We might have some DMT coming in next week if you're interested,' Blake says. 'Working on a new link.'

'Oh yeah? Safe, man, sounds good. I'll take some for myself even if I can't push it.'

'Yeah, that shit's crazy bro. Well, I'll text you when we get it in.'

'Safe, cheers man.'

'I'll drop you here at the lights.'

He slows to a stop at the junction. Wipers clear the rain, and the red light's vivid through the window for a second before rain obscures it again.

'Cheers, guys.'

'Calm.'

They offer their fists and I bump them again before I climb out. The light turns amber then green and it takes them a second to drive away. An impatient man in the Audi behind them leans on his horn, and they speed away.

He wouldn't have done that if he had any idea who they were, if he knew about the strap in the car. Maybe even two.

Mum's in the kitchen listening to the radio or some podcast with the kettle boiling. I slip past and go in my room, lock the door just to be safe, and lay my new stock out on my desk.

I put my alt-elect playlist on, roll a zoot, then get to work.

Good little stash this. Should be good for a few weeks, maybe a month. Few grand in profit.

I go in my closet for the baggies, scale, and additives. Start with the weed. Got a few Qs left in the stash, so I break two of the Os down into Qs, turn the rest into 3.5s and twenty bags.

Haven't heard from Mina for a couple weeks. Maybe she hasn't been smoking so much. Or might be picking up from someone else. Suits me just fine either way.

Roll another joint, change the music for some downtempo shit. Brings the ache into the foreground, but it's a vibe. Comforting almost.

Let's get this over with. Then maybe play some guitar. Might order a takeaway later.

I grab the printer paper box lid from my closet and pour the coke into it, then add the caffeine and Persil powder, mix it up with my old debit card. Weigh it out into gram bags and eightballs.

I grab my mortar and pour the MD in, crush it up nice and fine with the pestle, mix in the additives, then bag it up while smoking my joint.

Just the pills now. Nice and easy. Split them into ones, twos, fives, and tens, and bag them up too. Transfer the new stuff to the right compartments of my stash bag.

Yeah, all nicely stocked now. Plenty of acid and ket left, and a few grams of mushrooms left, although I'll probably save them for myself until I can restock. Hopefully get that DMT next week too. Man, it's been a while. Think I'll do a solo trip when it comes in. Go to space for a minute. Nothing compares. The memory's so dreamlike. But I know it was real.

Maybe Dimitri will resolve some things for me. Give me some perspective.

Fall back into my chair. Look around. Feel kind of empty beneath the buzzing high.

Alone.

Yeah, I'll order food in a minute. Where's my bong?

Watch the breath amidst the chaos. Forget the noise and the pain and the grinding ache in your soul.

Inhale. Exhale.

Watching the breath.

Inhale.Exhale. In awareness.

Watching the watching of the breath.

Who is?

Inhale exhale inhale exhale.

Watching the watching of the watching of the breath.

Don't want to think. Don't want to feel.

Then don't. Stay with it, Sam.

Watching the watching the watching the watching the breath. Watching watching watching watching.

Hey you. How you doing? Feels like I haven't seen you in ages.

Yeah, I've just been busy you know. Uni and shit.

Yeah I feel you man. You want to chill for a minute? Smoke one.

Sure.

I lead her upstairs and she sits on my bed. I hand her the three-five and she hands over the cash.

Here.

She offers me a nug from the bag.

I wave it away.

Don't worry. I'll roll from my supply.

You sure?

Yeah. Come on, I've got no shortage of weed. And I get it cheaper. You keep that for later.

Alright, thanks, Sam.

So what about you? How's things? How's your art?

Oh, yeah, it's good. I mean, I don't know, I've been in a bit of a funk recently. But I've been painting lots. Spent most of my last paycheque on new paints and canvases. But it's good. I like the stuff. So I can't complain. And Dom has a friend who might be able to get me a spot at an exhibition in a few weeks that's themed around connection. My stuff's probably a bit out there compared to the other artists, but I think a couple of my paintings would fit the theme, and I'm trying to do something new for it. If they accept me. I don't know.

They'd be crazy not to. Your work's amazing.

Well, it's all subjective, but thanks. I don't want to get my hopes up. I think it's just some guy that went to Dom's school. These things can sometimes be a bit nepotistic you know, a bit in-crowd. But we'll see.

Yeah, well fingers crossed. If they're really about their art, it should be a no-brainer.

Thanks.

I get the joint lit, hit it a few times, pass it.

How is he? Dom I mean.

Oh. Yeah. He's good. He's looking at getting a car soon, so we'll be able to go on road trips during the summer.

Oh, nice, sounds good.

You should come. We were thinking about going wild camping somewhere, maybe doing mushrooms or something. Ella's down.

Maybe. I'll have to see what I'm doing closer to the time.

Alright, cool man. Yeah, I'll let you know.

She leans back against my pillows, exhales. Smoke obscures the light, then disperses.

I mean we have been fighting more lately, but I know he's just stressed about his family stuff.

Oh yeah? What's happened?

Mm. Well it's just his dad as usual. He treats his mum like shit, always shouting at her and putting her down. She wants them to see a marriage counsellor, but he doesn't think anything's wrong. He was always nice around me, but I think he was just putting that on. And I've seen him get angry a few times. Dom doesn't take me round anymore. Basically, his dad's an arsehole.

She leans forward and passes the joint.

Yeah, join the club.

You too?

Mm.

I ash the joint and take a long drag.

Thankfully he fucked off when I was seven, moved up north with this woman he was having an affair with. But he used to abuse Mum. I don't have very good memories of him. But hey, he's someone else's problem now.

I'm sorry. That must have been really hard for you.

Ah what can you do? No one chooses their parents. Some people get a good hand, others get a heap of shit. I had it easy compared to a lot of people.

Yeah, but it still has an effect. I mean you're a lovely guy and I wouldn't have guessed you had a shitty dad, but you know everything has an effect on how we see the world, even in subtle ways.

It's true. I think that's why I'm drawn to psychology, exploring the mind and trying to make sense of those little things that most people don't even question. Just go their whole life thinking 'this is reality' and they live their days with those fundamental distortions colouring their whole experience of the world.

Yeah man. Like Dom's a good guy deep down, and I know he loves me, but sometimes I don't think he questions these things and just gets caught up in his emotions and his temper.

People are messy.

I'll drink to that.

She smiles as I pass the joint back. Her gaze lingers on the Alex Grey print, like some deep truth is veiled in the shape and colour, before she comes back to herself, raises the joint to her lips.

Her phone vibrates and she stares at the screen for a moment.

El wants to go out tomorrow. There's another house party. You wanna come?

Erm.

Part of me does, but do I want a repeat of last time? It was mostly my own doing, but I don't want to feel like that. Was two weeks away enough? It felt alright, but being around her again brings everything back. I'll just go out with the guys.

Actually I have plans.

Aw, that sucks. Well another time. It's always a good night with you.

Yeah. I'm sure you'll have a good time with the girls.

Yeah. In that case, I should probably get some other shit. You got Molly and coke?

Yeah. What do you want?

Um. A gram of each?

Sure.

I go to the closet and get gram baggies of MD and coke. The new shit. She doesn't get my private cleaner product. When we're partying together, I'm happy to share, but I still need to make my profit.

Oh, shit. I only have another twenty quid. I could bank transfer you the rest?

Don't worry about it. You can give me the rest next time you pick up weed or whatever.

Alright. Thanks, Sam.

She puts the drugs away in her bag and passes the joint.

That's a perk to having a good friend as a dealer. Like normally I'd be worried about meeting a dealer on my own. Sometimes they can be creepy and that. And it's not like you can go to the police if they do anything. So I'd just get a guy to pick up for me. But I trust you. I always feel safe around you.

I thought he was okay. I thought he was safe. A good bhikkhu. But he's fucking crazy. Left me to die. Or maybe he's still there, sitting, waiting on the other side of the door. A half-smile on his face as he listens to me sighing and groaning to myself.

Why would you do this to me?

Life is suffering. Isn't that what us Buddhists believe?

It doesn't mean it like that. You just want me to suffer for your own sick pleasure.

Someone must notice I'm missing by now. The other bhikkhus. The Ajahns. Unless… But of course. They're in on it too. They probably put Rich up to it. All conspiring against me. They'll have told the sangha I just went home. Or I'm away temporarily on community service.

Am I the only one? Or are there other bhikkhus trapped in their rooms right now? Pissing in bottles and shitting in corners. Starving and thirsting, wasting away. Initiations into some twisted cult.

It's all for your own good. You came here for enlightenment, didn't you? You need to suffer first. Only then in the darkest dark will you see the light.

It's just sadistic. What a fucking joke.

I hammer on the door.

'Rich. Rich, let me out of here right now. I quit. I'm done with this shit. Fuck your enlightenment. Fuck nibbāna.'

No response.

'Rich, open this door, or I'm going to kick the fucking thing down.'

I rear back against the window and kick the door. Again. Again. Again.

Not enough space to get any real momentum. And I'm weak, muscles all atrophied after so many weeks of rice and green tea and withdrawal sweats and sitting in meditation and slaving around doing maintenance work around the monastery.

All part of the plan.

I kick again. Throw my shoulder against the door but it only results in new pains and my muscles all ache and breath comes thick and fast so I sit on my bunk, pull my knees to my chest and just focus on catching my breath.

The sky outside is bright and a little overcast. The trees just invading the frame sway in a light breeze. In any other circumstances, a rather serene view. Maybe it's not so bad. If I conserve my energy, I can last a few days maybe. They say you can live about three days without water, but that'll be an average, probably based on people going about their lives, using up a normal day's energy. If I sit in meditation, bring my energy all the way down, still my thoughts - that uses up a lot - I can probably survive at least a week. There are stories of bodhisattas sitting for weeks in meditation. Their blood and their breath slowing so they look dead to all appearances. People would step over them in the streets, empty their pockets.

No. That's what they want. Then they win. You can't let them violate you like this. You have to rage. Fight. Smash the glass out the window and drag yourself through, you can fit, just watch the edges. Take a shard with you and kill any man who tries to stop you.

I can't. I don't have the energy yet.

Wait. Rest for a minute. Then when you have your breath, do it. Don't hold back. Your life depends on it.

Inhalexhaleinhale.

Close my eyes.

Try to slow the breath. Inhale. Exhale.

Inhale.

Exhale.

Fucking kill him. He can't do this to me.

Blood running. Until his breath stops. I'll make him pay. Before I escape.

Thinking. Be calm, Sam. Focus on the breath. Inhale. Exhale.

Flickers of light, shimmering, shifting darkness behind my closed eyes.

Inhale.

Exhale.

Sam.

Inhale.

Sam, I'm scared.

It'll be fine. You're gonna be okay.

Screaming   screaming   screaming   screaming.
Shutthefuckup. Wasting my breath. Wasting my energy. The
end getting closer and closer and it can't be happening. It's
not supposed to be like this.

Sam.

What's up?

I'm so fucked up man.

Oh yeah? Having a good night?

No, I mean I don't feel good. I think I did too much
Molly. And coke.

Oh, right. Shit, sorry to hear that. Where are you?

Still outside the club. El's trying to get us a taxi.

Alright, cool. That's good. Yeah, just go home and rest.
Drink some water, but not too much.

I know. I have been, but I still feel too hot. Like I'm
burning up. I've never been this high before man. Is this
normal?

You'll be okay. Just get yourself home, have a can of
Coke or something, then get a cool flannel on your head.
Then just take it easy and you'll feel better soon.

Alright. I hope so. El, what's happening?

You okay? What's up?

Okay, the taxi's coming now. Sorry about this. It's
probably not how you want to spend your Saturday night.

No, don't be silly. I'm glad you called. You'll be okay.
I've been fucked up too bad a bunch of times myself. It can
be scary, but once you ride it out, you can laugh about it.
You always hear stories about how people go to the hospital
because they smoked too much or a guy in a K hole whose
friends have dumped him so some stranger panics and calls
an ambulance. How much did you take anyway?

Um, I don't know. I took a bomb of MD. Then we did
lines in the bathroom a few times and were keying more
MD. We went through the Molly and half the coke with
three of us.

What about drink?

Not a lot. A couple of beers. Few spirits.

Yeah, it's probably a big high, but you'll start coming down soon. Just get home and make yourself comfortable.

Man, and my head's killing me. El was giving me a head massage and that was helping but - hang on, I think the taxi's here.

Okay, cool. That's good.

God, I'm starting to feel sick too. I really hope I'm not sick in the taxi. Will you stay on the line with me?

Yeah, of course.

Heavy mouth breathing. Ella talking to the driver.

The car engine going and a girl, probably Cat talking to El in hushed voices.

She's going home. She's gonna be fine. Just pop a couple paracetamol, get a little sugar in you for the return journey. I'd smoke a joint, maybe even drop a Valium, but she doesn't have the tolerance to everything I do.

Oh yeah, she's fine. She's just really tired. Needs her bed you know. She's not gonna be sick, are you Meens?

No, I'm fine. Don't… don't worry. I'm just really hot still. Can we have the window open?

You okay?

I don't know, it's better, but I still don't feel good.

Is anyone going with you?

Yeah, Cat and El.

Like they're gonna stay with you?

Yeah, Ella is. I just hope my dad's not around.

Okay, cool. Yeah, probably just open the windows, get a cool flannel or something. Cool yourself down. But don't get an ice pack. You don't want to do it too quickly.

Alright. Yeah. Then I'll be alright? You don't think I should go to the hospital?

I mean I'm not there. I can't make the choice for you. But I've felt shitty like that a few times and I was fine. Just a nasty comedown, but it wore off. It's good that Ella's gonna stay with you.

Yeah. I'm tired. Just want to be in my bed.

Laughs.

You will be soon. Are you just coming from Greenwich?

No, we're…

Mina?

Sam, I really don't feel well. I just need to sleep, but my body has too much energy.

What's wrong with her?

She's alright. Don't worry.

Doesn't sound alright.

Yeah, it's a bitch. Are you nearly home now?

No, we're like ten minutes away still.

Oh okay. Well, just sit tight.

Yeah. I'm trying. Shit.

What? What's up?

Just my battery's gonna die soon.

Ah. Well you can plug it in when you get home and ring me back if you want to.

Yeah. Thanks, Sam. I'm sorry for ruining your night like this.

No, don't be silly. You haven't. Did you have a good time, before this I mean?

Not really. Me and Dom had a big fight again. I think that's why I… Jesus, my legs are shaking. You ever get that?

Yeah, a few times with weed, but I think that was more an anxiety thing. You had anxiety attacks before?

Not really. Not like this.

Heavy breathing.

Sam, I don't think this is normal. I think something's wrong.

What's wrong with her? You need to go to the hospital, love?

I don't know. Maybe. What do you think, El?

I mean it's probably better safe than sorry. If that's what you want.

I don't know, Sam, are you sure this is normal? I just really -

Mina? Are you still there?

Mina?

He's here.

I jerk around, but can't make sense of the darkness. Look for movement shifting against the fuzzy black mess.

You wouldn't know if he was. He could already be here. Waiting in a corner for the right moment. Or a vicious dog. Snakes slithering across the floor. And he would. He'd do it and much worse.

I jump, slapping my leg, but it's just an insect. Probably.

Can't stand it. Fucking hate this shit. It was better with the light on, with the videos playing.

The noise from the speakers vibrates my skull. I grit my teeth against it, but it just makes the pain worse.

I'm sorry. I could have prevented it. I know I could. I'm sorry. But it won't bring you back. He won't suffer any less because of it. Please, just make him stop. You know I liked you. You know I cared about you. If I'd known, I never would have done it. Just make him stop, please.

I can't do that.

Everything happens for a reason.

Fuck that. That's just something people say, and it's bullshit. There isn't meaning in this. This is just sadism. He's fucking insane.

I'm losing my mind. Probably lost it already. But still can't escape it.

Just want the noise to stop. If it was quiet, then I could put up with all the rest. All the pain and the sickness and delirium. I'd eat cat food and shit in corners. And be blind for the rest of my days. But at least it would be quiet. At least I could be mindful, go out with some small sense of dignity.

If only. If only.

What if you're wrong? What if you're so accustomed to the noise, it'll be worse once it's gone?

Fuck that. I could never get used to it. If only I could tune it out. Tune it all out. Just lose myself inside my mind.

But not this. Not her. Back to childhood. Back to the dream.

Just want to sleep. Maybe if I still my mind, I could for a minute. But sometime it's worse. Trying to sleep knowing it won't come. Torturing myself. So fucking exhausted. My muscles aching from misuse, and shifting my position helps only for a second before the pain consumes it again.

Should eat some more. I'll die if I don't. Wish I would. But you don't really. Eat it, Sam. It's not so bad.

Eat it, you fucking animal.

Reach along the wall for the tin, smell it in the darkness. Why? I know what it is. Dig my fingers in and lift the meaty jelly to my lips and chew.

Imagine it's something else. The bottom of a fatty stew. Then what's the jelly? Just like a stock pot. Old coagulated gravy.

The slime clings to my teeth and lines my throat when I swallow. Nothing to wash it down. All of it nauseatingly soft. My teeth weren't made for this.

More. Down the hatch. Chunks of chicken and jelly. Just a stew. But I know it's not. You don't care. You need it. It's not so bad. Just my stomach doesn't like it. Keep it down. You won't get any more. And I'm starving. So fucking hungry. I keep going. At least it gives me something to focus on that's not the distorted noise and the hard ground against my bones. And then I'm scraping the bottom of the tin, and it's all gone. I lick my fingers and toss the can towards the black corner. Don't even hear it land amidst the screaming. And now nothing else to do. Just lie here and absorb the nightmare, the endless assault on my every sense. And no end to it.

It must end at some point. Feels so far away, some celestial distance, but it's in the room too. Death. Waiting patiently for its time.

She's dead. She's dead and it's my fault. No, not my fault. She took too much. Someone must have cut the powder with some nasty shit. Not just caffeine and washing powder.

You sold them to her. They're gonna come for you when they find out. They'll do an autopsy. They'll ask questions. Where did she get the drugs? Her parents won't know anything probably. But friends. Ella knows. Cat. Dom. Maybe some others.

I need to get rid of the evidence. If they get a warrant to search the house or Mum lets them in, they'll find everything.

I go in the closet and get my bags. The stash and the rest of it. Baggies, additives, scales, tray. Can't leave a trace of it. And the cash. Especially the cash. I couldn't explain it. Not more than a couple hundred.

I should ditch the product. Somewhere far away. Somewhere they won't find it. But there's maybe a grand's worth here. It'd be like burning money. Maybe I could sell it on in bulk. Obviously not the MD and coke. I need to get rid of those just in case. Could I find a buyer for the rest at such short notice? And it'd still be risky.

Forget the drugs. But I'll bury the cash somewhere. In the garden while Mum's at work. They wouldn't dig up the garden looking for evidence. I can get it back once things have died down.

Where to ditch the bags? Nowhere close by. It's too busy. Someone would find them sooner or later. And I can't just dig up patches of grass in the city.

A dumpster maybe. A big commercial one for a restaurant or shop or something. But even then, there's a chance someone would get curious and look inside. Take it for themselves if they're smart, report it to the feds if not. And then they've got my prints all over everything.

Open Google Maps and stare, hoping for inspiration to strike. Come on, Sam, we don't have time to waste. Rivers are no good. But a lake maybe. Hyde Park. The Serpentine? It's far enough away. Quite public still, but not at night. It's either that or get a train way out of London. Somewhere rural. I'd have to wait until daylight, and I don't have time for that shit. It needs to be gone tonight. I can taxi it to

North Greenwich, get the night tube into central. Bury the cash when I come back.

While I wait for the taxi, I scour my room for any other evidence. There's my private weed stash and all my rolling stuff. Can't get rid of that. I won't make it through the next few days without being able to smoke. Even if they did find a few grams of weed, what's the worst that would happen?

I hide it in a smell-proof bag inside Russian dolls of boxes in the back of my closet.

The park's still lit by streetlights. A few teenage boys sit on a bench passing a joint between them. A couple pass by further up. Odd clusters of drunks taking a shortcut through the park after a night out.

I light another cigarette, head for the lake. Only two left. I'll need to find an open shop and buy more for tonight. Can't see myself being able to sleep. Don't want to sleep.

Don't deserve to.

I can drop the bags off the bridge when no one's around, but I need to weigh them down to make sure they sink. Should have thought about that before. I'll have to find something. Rocks or bits of wood or something. Bricks would be best, but I'm not going back now.

I head into the trees and use my phone torch to light the way. Deeper in, I spot a few good candidates. Unzip the bags and load them with the heaviest sticks and rocks I find. Takes me a few minutes before both bags are full and hefty. No way they'll stay afloat now.

I should save some acid. The coke and Molly and ket I can live without, but the psychs, it hurts to see them go. So many good memories. And they've helped me through so many bad experiences.

Is it really worth a prison sentence? You can always buy more. You know half a dozen dealers you can buy more from.

Fuck it.

I emerge from the trees and head for the bridge. The

bags heavy now. Arms and shoulders aching. Another couple walking in front. I slow my pace, then linger in the middle, wait a couple of minutes for a solo dog walker to pass. They must be out of earshot now. But the bags will make a big splash. Maybe another minute just to be safe. But then I risk someone else coming out of the darkness.

I finish the cigarette. Light another. Just one left now.

It's now or never. Do it.

I hurl the bags over the edge and they hit the water one just after the other in a flam, throwing up a spray of water, then sinking. Out of sight, but the ripples still spreading.

I turn and walk back the way I came, pulling my hood lower over my face and sucking on the cigarette.

How are you doing?

I don't know man. I still can't believe it, you know. Like there must have been a mistake. I'm back home now, and the comedown's hitting. I've never felt like this before.

You don't feel sick like she did?

Nah. I mean I feel like shit, but I'll be okay physically. I just can't believe it man. Just like that. And it's my fault. I should have slowed her down. She was just upset about Dom, and I wanted to get fucked up too.

Crying.

Hey, it's not your fault.

You see stories on the news, but you never think it'll be you. Or your friends.

I know. It's awful. She was a really good person.

It's too fucking soon man. It's not fair.

I know. I'm sorry. But listen, El, you can't tell the police anything if they ask you, okay? Just say you don't know about any drugs. She must have got them in the club.

Really, Sam? Her body's not even cold yet and that's all you fucking care about, covering your own back?

Hey, come on. I'm torn up about it as well. I know you go way back, but I liked her too. I'm distraught about it too, but they could put me away for life if anyone talks. And I don't deserve that. I didn't do anything. A second life ruined isn't going to help anyone.

Do you think I'm stupid, man? Obviously I'm not going to talk. I was taking shit just like her.

Okay, thanks, El. It means a lot. What about Cat?

She didn't take anything. She was just drinking.

But would she talk? Can you tell her not to say anything? Just say she must have got any drugs at the club? For your own peace of mind too.

Jesus, Sam. Yes, I'll talk to her. She'll keep her mouth shut, okay?

Yeah, I… thank you.

I should go. I just want to be alone.

Alright. No worries. I'll let you be. But hey, I'm here if you ever want to talk about it.

…Yeah.

Need to shit. Can't put it off any longer.

I push myself to my knees, muscles weak and atrophying, feel around for the wall, shuffle forward until the shackle pinches my raw ankle.

Get to my feet, turn my back to the corner, legs trembling, so weak, the smell of piss already hitting me. Barely push and the shit falls out of me, half of it water, splashes the back of my ankles. My stomach bubbles and aches as more comes. I need to piss too, aim my dick back, but only a dribble comes out. My head pounding with the incessant drums and distorted guitars that stopped sounding like guitars a long time ago. Legs trembling, threatening to give up. Can't take anymore.

I drop forward onto my knees, and my arms are too weak to catch me, fall face first and hit my chin on the tiles. Lie there splayed on the cold floor just breathing. Inhale-exhale-inhale. Competing for attention, my overworked heart dum-dum-dum-dum-dum-dum-dum. Still feel the wetness on my ankles. Smell my own inhuman shit and piss mixing with sweat and puss and whatever the fuck else.

This is life now. This is what it means to be.

And you deserve it all.

That's not fair. No one deserves this. No one.

The despair rises in me, but can't cry. I would, it might feel good, but my body won't allow it. Can't spare the fluid.

And you don't get to feel better. You don't get your catharsis.

My knees ache from the pressure. My sore jaw still singing over the music. Roll over onto my shoulder, then my back. Turning over and over and over, the hard ground against shoulders, back, and chest.

Only darkness around me.

Wish he'd come up and slit my throat. End it nice and quick. It'd be the least he could do. Then maybe I'd forgive him. If he took it all away. I've suffered like you have. Now let it go. This can't go on forever.

What is forever?

It'll go on as long as you wish it.

Lost in my mind again. Thoughts and feelings and sensations. So hard not to.

I know. But this is not you.

Breathe.

My last energy still dutifully working the lungs. The breath which has never failed me before. Euphoria glimmers for a second, gone without a trace in the next. A star blinking one final time before it's swallowed by the dark.

No, please. Don't I deserve even that? Just a little relief, a little positive feeling to counteract all this pain and misery? Now that it's gone so quickly, I wish I'd never glimpsed it. Just tortures me all the more.

Remember when you didn't want to die?

You do this to yourself.

Probably a neuronal glitch. Maybe there'll be more as my body fails me. Maybe right on the edge, my brain will dump all its neurotransmitters, dopamine and endogenous hallucinogens. One last trip to see me through to the other side.

Other side? Of what?

The darkness changes shape, a shifting grey amidst the black, then the light attacks. I raise my arm to shield my eyes but I need to look, need to see what's coming. He walks to the wall, carrying something. A free-standing fan. I take long blinks, each exposure to the light stabbing my eyes. The room's bigger than I remember. Or I'm smaller. It's been so long since I saw it. Still the chair lying in the middle of the room. The horrific mess of shit and piss in the corner. My dirty, yellowed skin. My ankle looks infected where the cuff's chafed it. A pus-filled welt forming. Maybe a bug got me. I know they're down here. My knuckles dried with blood from hitting the wall.

That was ages ago.

What is time to you?

He plugs the fan into the wall where the laptop charger was, turns it on, locks the rotation, and aims it down at me. Retreats back out of the room without looking at me. Leaves the light on and the door an inch open.

My heart jumps. A chance.

I jerk at the cuff, but it stings my ankle.

You've tried that.

The air's cold on my skin.

I grab the cat food tin. Whiskas. Hammer at the chain. Fucking useless. What, did you think you were going to break it like that? But I have to do something. I won't get another chance.

There's nothing to do. If there was, I'd have done it already.

Doesn't matter now. He's back with another big fan. Jesus Christ. He plugs it in the opposite wall, aims it at me, turns it on.

Two currents blasting cold air at me. Like I wasn't cold enough already. Two sentinels stationed to ensure my continued torment.

He looks at me, and I instinctively cross a leg over my dick.

Like you have any pride left.

He's so tall. Looks stronger than before. Maybe I'm just weaker. Definitely weaker.

He grimaces at the smell or maybe the noise, glares at me with a mix of hatred and sick pleasure at seeing me so pathetic and helpless. I shiver against the cold, grows to a painful tremor in my legs, then ebbs away to a general shaking. The vibration of my body with the distorted screaming.

'You'll kill me.'

He smiles, presses a hand to his ear.

I'll die if my temperature drops too low.

Isn't that what you want? A quicker end.

'You don't want me to die yet.'

He frowns, shrugs, then heads out, killing the light on the way.

A level deeper in hell. I hug my arms around myself, stroke my arms. I'm so exhausted, it's hard to tell the difference between the tiredness and the incessant low-level nausea. My body shakes violently and I hit my head against the wall a couple of times to stop it.

Any rare hope of sleep eradicated by the immediate discomfort of the cold. Not just discomfort. Already starting to feel like a dull burn. In the dark, how do I know the difference between cold and heat?

I shuffle a few inches down the wall, but it makes no difference. I can't escape the two monsters. Breathing heavy again. Wasting energy. Lost in thought. Awareness abandoned in some other realm.

I hold my head in my hands and scream a long, silent scream, its only feedback the tension in my face and my aching jaw.

I could kill myself. I should kill myself. It'd solve all my problems, not least of all the existential one.

It's only right. Karma.

Jump off one of the high bridges. Something quick and painless. Couldn't cut my wrists. Or just take a massive cocktail of drugs in a bomb and a bunch of diazepams. I'd pass out and never wake up. But all my drugs are at the bottom of the Serpentine. Should have kept some behind. I could buy some more. I could have them in a few hours.

Not yet. Jesus, I'm on the edge of acting. Not just some abstract fantasy. It could move me to do it just as easily as the thought passes through my mind.

Need to calm myself down. Smoke some.

I go to the window and watch the street for a minute to make sure no one's watching, then go in the closet and hunt for my weed stuff. Roll a joint with trembling fingers. The same fingers that would grip a paring knife from the kitchen drawer, trace down the veins in my forearms.

There should be pain. It's only right.

Spark the joint, pace the room. I should go for a walk just to let out some energy. But what if my feet guide me to some high place and over the edge?

I shouldn't do it where someone will find me. It has to be out of the way. No one else needs to suffer from my actions.

And what about the people who will suffer from your death? While you slip away from guilt and responsibility, what will Mum suffer? Friends and family? Neighbours? Coursemates? It'd destroy Mum. She has no one else. What has she done to deserve that?

That's you, always looking for the easy way out.

And what if I end up in prison? That'll break her too.

You won't. No one will talk. The coroner will chalk it up to another nightlife casualty and police won't do shit.

It might actually be okay. I might get away with it. But that's probably worse than getting caught. Don't I deserve some kind of retribution?

Come on, man. You didn't cut the shit. Not with anything bad. It must have been Blake and James or their supplier or theirs. Or a few of them combined, all thinking their additives wouldn't hurt but all together amounting to a lethal dose.

If I knew who it was, I'd kill them myself. That'd be justice. But there's no point me losing my life over it. Yeah. That's right. The weed and tobacco calming me down a bit now. It'd be crazy to kill myself. What the fuck was I thinking?

Just need to sit tight. But every day watching the windows, waiting for a hammer on the door. Flashing lights. Or some lone stranger in the shadow of night. A knife at my throat.

No one's coming.

But I don't know that until they don't come, and until then, I can only wait. Can't run or they'll get suspicious. And they can still get me if I run. Better to hunker down here and just wait it out. I need to get more weed. It's a risk if they're watching me, but I need it to see me through. I'll lose my mind without it.

Second phone vibrates. People wanting to link. Didn't they get my message?

People need their drugs. Well they'll have to get them elsewhere for now. I could maybe give a few of them Jake's number. The regular stoners. He'd be grateful for the extra Ps, and they're good customers. Or someone else will fill the void.

And then how will I make money? I guess I have money to see me through uni. Hopefully I'll get a proper job. That's if I haven't fucked this year completely. As long as I've got money, I'll be alright.

That's your fucking problem.

You can't survive without money in this world. Otherwise you're nothing. You're no one.

Root of evil though. Look where it's led you.

I turn off my burner. Message Jake. He's gotta be about tonight. I can just swing by his. Not for a few hours probably.

I roll again.

Do you think your upbringing affected your creativity? Not just the content of your art but like your emotional reactions and your passion for it?

I don't know. I guess.

Like I don't know if it's necessarily a compulsion for you, but something drives us to be creative, you know. Or maybe a bunch of things interact and motivate us to pick up the paintbrush or the guitar or whatever it is. Like for me, playing guitar is a way of releasing energy. It calms me down. Even if the stuff I'm playing is pretty heavy and intense, it's like I burn a lot of energy in the physicality but also the emotion of it, and then when I'm finished playing, my mind feels clearer.

That's cool.

What about you? What guides your drawing?

I don't know. It's not that deep to be honest. I just sketch sometimes when I'm bored. I haven't painted anything really good since A-level art.

Her friend walks up, touches her arm.

I need another drink. You coming?

Sure.

They turn away and head into the mass of slowly writhing bodies, gone like they were never here to start with. Standing on my own. Could get another drink myself, but my body protests. The pleasant warmth is becoming uncomfortable. Burning up. Should get some air.

I head out the front, light a cigarette. That's nice, the breeze flirting with the internal warmth and me somewhere in between. Body's pretty numb, legs like jelly.

I slide down the wall and sit smoking, watching the neon signs across the street, alternating between two frames, the cocktail glass blinking in and out of existence. Playing hide and seek. Here, now gone, now here, now gone. Ebb and flow of euphoria but the horrible malaise lurking behind it. Just waiting for me to come down so it can consume me whole. Pin me in bed for another few days like weighted blankets.

The outflow of people from the bars and clubs getting heavier now. Heading to fast food joints or back home to fuck before they pass out. Wake up with shame and bedridden from the hangover or comedown. But none of them worse than me. We're all heading down the same pit but me so much deeper and no glimpse of climbing out without more drugs.

Not yet. Let me stay high just a little longer. I dig my baggie and keys out of my pocket, do another key up each nostril. I'll smoke a joint when I get in to soften the comedown. Should have enough to see me through the day.

Yeah, that's it. The cool air on my skin. All my neurons singing in harmony. This is it. Everything else is just a distraction or an attempt to get here. People waste their lives chasing power and fame and love and piety. But this moment right here, this is it.

My eyes close for a moment and the colours swim lazily in the sea of proximal darkness, distinct but always a suggestion of coalescence. Ultimately the same but playing at being different for the moment. Even the static humming of my body suggests some secret affinity with the shape and colour.

The cigarette drops from my lips into my lap.

Guys laughing. Youthful ignorance of the world and its jagged edges. Or maybe they know the meaningless of it all and tonight just a distraction from the weight of it.

You alright mate?

Try to open my eyes but I can't. Try to at least nod but can't manage that either.

He's fucked up man.

Someone's had a good night.

Yo let's get a taxi before they close bro. The queue's already mad.

Aite… Take it easy dude.

Much closer now. He pats me on the head. But I'm not

really here.

Need to get home. Can't just sit here in the street. It'll get dangerous. They can do anything to my body without me to protect it.

It's not you. You don't really need it. All you need is this feeling here.

Just need to get home. Get myself in a taxi. Then I can drift off for a bit.

Can't move a muscle. The frayed tether between me and my body already out of reach.

Are you alright?

A girl now. Her voice husky and a little rough. Essex. But beautiful. Even without seeing her, I know there's a Goddess in her. If I could speak I'd tell her. But all I manage is a couple of meaningless throat noises. A sleeper grumbling to themselves.

Hey, do you know this guy? Is he with you?

Nah. He's been sitting there a while.

Hey, are you okay?

Touching my arm. My forehead.

He's really hot.

Probably fucked on drugs. Let's get out of here.

We can't just leave him. He doesn't look good. He needs help.

What do you wanna do?

We should call an ambulance.

They'll take like an hour at this time of night. I thought we were getting a Maccies.

Well go if you want. I'll meet you later. But I'm not just leaving him here. I'm calling an ambulance.

Don't. Just leave me. But I can't communicate with her. A heavy veil between us, separating my world from theirs.

Waves crashing, floating above it, like a camera angle pulling up and out of my body. This here perfect and pure but my body frozen in the depths below.

Dial tone ringing.

Hello? Yeah, ambulance please.

Just leave me. I'll be fine in an hour or two. Don't get an ambulance out. They might bring police. I've still got product on me. They'll throw me in a cell to await my judgement in the morning when I come down.

Try to tell her. Just speak for a few seconds to tell her I'm fine, but I can't even murmur now. The silence is so blissful, it's hard to focus on the distant sounds and sensations. I just want to go out like a light and be this awareness and nothing else.

I don't know. Let me check.

She presses her fingers against his neck - my neck.

Yeah there's a pulse but it's slow. And he's breathing but slowly too. He can't open his eyes... I don't know. I don't know him. We just found him here... Okay.

The music gets louder for a moment as the door opens. Reminds me of something. So vivid like a portal into that world is just waiting to open up. It's there, so close, but then it's muffled again, and I can't hear it, and the echo is already fading in this space. What was the song?

She says something else but her voice is too echoey and the soft ringing drowns her out. Like a bell. Yes, like a wand tracing the rim. Round and round and round. An infinite ringing as long as there is life to produce it, growing louder, heralding the appearance of something long-forgotten. A losing but also a finding. A place where even the warm, euphoric glow subsides, and there's only silence. The faintest ripples of vibration fading away. Infinite nothingness.

Inhale...Exhale...

Inhale.

Distant sirens. But not so distant. Not from him.

About fucking time.

It's alright mate, the ambulance is coming.

Wish she'd shut up. Wish all the noise and distractions

would fade again. I only want to float. Drift off in the breeze to where she is.

Mina.

Yes, but the greater her. The infinite, divine feminine. The birthplace of all creation.

You want to be a helpless little baby again, is that it? Too late for that shit. You can't ever go back. Just the grave to come for you now, and maybe sooner rather than later.

This him? What are we working with?

I just found him like that.

Do you know if he took anything?

I don't know. Like I told you, I don't know him.

Alright, let's have a look at you.

She touches his neck with latex fingertips. Feels the weak pulse. Leans close to his lips. Peels an eyelid open.

Woman's face staring at me through thick clouds. Neon Litchenberg figures superimposed. Then black again. It's me. This body is me. No it's not. That's what they want you to think. How can you be him when you can so easily leave him behind?

But that's all inside your mind.

I wouldn't be so sure.

What's your name, mate? Do you know his name?

No.

Listen, can we go? We've been waiting forever.

Yeah, yeah, we'll take it from here.

He's got a pulse and he's breathing, but we don't know what he's taken. Chances are he'll come back to himself soon enough, but we can't just leave him here.

Shall I get the stretcher?

Can you walk, mate?

He can't fucking walk. Look at him. Can't even open his eyes. I'll get the stretcher.

Hands roam in my pockets, take things out. My wallet. Drugs.

Hello. Naughty naughty. What do we have here? Think I'll keep that for later. I wouldn't mind a bit of whatever you're on. There's not much left though, you greedy bastard. You got any more?

Feeling in my pockets again. Brushing my cock.

Here, look what I found.

What is it?

Hm. Not sure. Tastes like cocaine. But could be ketamine. I guess we'll find out.

Yeah. Come on then, give me a hand.

They shift me onto the flat cushioned platform and then the air changes and the wheels squeak as we move.

More laughter.

Look at the fucking state of this guy.

That'll be you by the end of the night.

Fuck off.

Excuse me lads.

Then moving up. Sound echoing closer. The back of the ambulance. The door slams, and I jump but don't actually move a muscle. Nasty disorientating feeling. Here but also not. The engine starts, changes pitch as the ambulance moves. Slip slowly backwards. My stomach filling with nausea. Can't see anything. Flat on my back. If I vomit now, it'll stop in my throat. The irony of dying in the back of an ambulance. Happens all the time. Nothing ironic about it.

But I can't die now. It's not my time.

I thought that's what you wanted? Jump off a nice high bridge? Slit your wrists? Karma and all that.

Not like this.

It'll be fine. You'll separate from your body just like before, like you do every night when you sleep, except your body will shut down and there's no coming back.

Drifting forever.

Is that really the way?

Their voices in the cab. Can't hear them over the engine though. The vehicle accelerates fast and I slide back. My crown thuds against the ambulance doors, pain singing in my head, and my stomach harmonising. They didn't put the fucking brakes on the stretcher.

Too claustrophobic in here. I'm too big to be contained like this. Expansive consciousness. Too much like a coffin.

It's not you.

The ambulance brakes too fast and I slide again, my feet hitting the other wall. The engine slows, then cuts off. Doors open and close. The cold air cooling my skin. That's nice.

Get his feet.

The guy climbing up beside me.

That was quick.

They lift my big, dead weight. His warm, heavy breathing on my face. It's quiet. Just the faint sound of traffic.

Over there. Quick before someone sees.

What's happening? We can't be at the hospital yet.

I try to open my eyes, manage one. Still blurry and distorted, but I see him carrying me. We're by the road. On the bridge.

Hurry up. I can't hold him much longer.

By the edge. The Thames far below.

No. I'm aware. I can see. Look at me. Please.

They don't care. It's too late for that shit.

On three.

Quickly.

One, two, three.

Falling falling falling, almost feels pleasant, then the ground smashes into my back. Not ground. Water. Sinking sinking. The air gone from my lungs but no hope of getting it back. Only water slipping in. Can't move a muscle, even now.

You did this.

Sinking sinking.

Laughing.

Sinking.

Splitting.

Sinking.

Separating.

Sinking.

The light snaps on and I have to contend with the assault on my retinas and the panic spurring my body. The overlapping music still raging on.

He takes his phone out of his pocket, taps the screen a few times, and the music ceases. Silence swells. Oh God, it's been so long since I heard it. My ear drums flexing like plastic in heat. Ringing.

He looks angry. Probably drunk. He shuts off both fans, then sets a Sainsbury's bag on the chair, takes out a plastic water bottle, and slowly offers it to me.

Is it a trick?

I take it.

'Thank you.'

'Drink.'

I unscrew the cap, and tip the bottle back. The cool water reawakens the feeling in my mouth and throat. That's good. Drain half the bottle and put the cap back on. Throat still sore and scratchy despite the water. Feels worse.

'Drink it. All of it.'

But I might not get anymore for God knows how long. Should ration it. But there's danger in his eyes.

I untwist the cap, finish the water in two big swallows.

He nods, takes a Heineken can out of the bag, and drinks from it. What else is in the bag?

'Nothing to say for yourself? Not so fucking chatty now, are you?'

What does he want me to say? What's left to say?

I just look at him.

'You disgust me, you know that? I can barely stand to look at you.'

Then don't. You did this. You're the reason I'm in this state.

That's not what he means.

'I'm sorry.'

'You're sorry. Yeah yeah. Like that means a fucking thing to me. It's too late for that.' He gulps his beer, fumbles in his pocket, and lights a cigarette. Catches the scent of the shit, grimaces, then glares at me with revulsion.

My legs still shaking. Maybe without the fans, they'll stop for a moment.

'Hurting me won't-'

'What?' Leans forward suddenly. I shrink back to the wall, and he scoffs.

'Hurting me won't change anything.'

'Well, it makes me feel a damn sight better.'

'I don't believe that.'

He stands up, kicks back the chair, scrapes against the tile. 'What the fuck do you know? Seeing you suffer is the only thing that keeps me going anymore. You think I don't know it won't bring them back? You think I give a shit? This isn't about them. This is about me.'

Them? What does he mean them?

He stares, equally confused for a second, then laughs manically to himself. 'You don't know, do you? No. No, you just fucked off to your little monastery and left the world behind to suffer from the shit you created.'

I wait for him to explain, but he just sucks on his cigarette, the fury building in his eyes. He seems to contemplate for a second, then steps forward, grabs my arm, and stabs the cigarette against my skin.

It burns and I try to pull away but he holds me too tight, still pressing with the cigarette and I already smell the burning skin. I grab hold of his arm for leverage, but it infuriates him all the more and he slaps me across the face. Straightens up and kicks me in the ribs. Again. I pull my limbs in to protect my torso, try to roll sideways, but my cuff won't let me.

Kicks me again in the arm. Punches me in the side of the head. Grabs my throat and squeezes, pins me against the wall.

'You fucking cunt. You murdering fucking cunt.'

I close my eyes to focus on not passing out. Head swimming with the pain and exhaustion.

'Look at me.'

I stare into his red, rageful face. His eyes searing like my arm. Nothing but hate.

It doesn't have to be this way. You don't have to do this.

He squeezes tighter, everything constricting in that deathly impetus. Ears ring and his face starts to blur, but he releases me, hits me hard again in the cheek. Pulls me back to my senses. He kicks me again, again. Walks away. Thank God. But he takes something from the shelving. A hammer. Comes back.

No please.

I try to dodge it, but he catches me on the elbow. The shoulder. Goes for my head but hits the wall. Grabs my arms so I can't block him properly. Holds the hammer above his head.

Please. Don't.

He turns and hurls it at the shelving unit. It knocks a box of screws onto the floor, spilling across the tiles.

'Fucking arsehole.' He fumbles in his pockets for another cigarette. Paces in front of me as he smokes. 'I should kill you. It's what you deserve.'

I can only breathe and hug myself, rub my arm between my elbow and shoulder. Everything hurting. The old aches and bruises nothing in comparison. My body groans and screams instead of my mouth. Not with him here. Just be still and silent. He'll go soon.

He remembers his beer, drains it, sits back in the chair and takes a long drag.

'I'll never get the image out of my head. Because of you. Lying on the bathroom floor like that. She killed herself because of you. Because you took our daughter from us. She was all we had. And now I've got nothing. All because of you.'

I don't say anything. There's nothing to say. Don't even rub the sores. Just let his pain and mine flow and the guilt repeatedly stab my gut.

I didn't know. It makes sense now. All the rage and the

suffering. I couldn't imagine his pain, but I don't need to because I feel it now. He made me feel it.

The silence exposes it all. No other noise or theatrics to hide it. Just his heavy breathing across the room and my own pathetic wheezing. The mess of the room we both made. He tosses his cigarette into the corner. Lights another. I stare at the ground, so tired, my eyes only half-open, and he stares at a spot not far from mine.

The pain my only possible object of meditation, forcing everything else from awareness. Time churns along as we sit with it, then starts to dissolve.

Sometime later, he rises and walks slowly, somnambulantly out. Doesn't look back. Doesn't switch the fans back on or kill the light. I sit there, waiting, waiting for the speakers to jolt to life and resume their familiar assault. But minutes pass, more.

I lean sideways and fall against the floor, the cold tile against my face and arm, curl up into a ball. A trickle of feeling, then a river, a flood. Energy I didn't think I had, energy reserved only for sorrow fills me and I cry for Mina, for her mother who sang her happy birthday a thousand times, who watched her school performances, and beamed at her daughter all grown up on prom night. I cry for my own mother, and for the other bhikkhus I'll never see again, and for him and for anyone who's ever lost someone.

It's okay, Sam.

It's not. It can't be okay. I deserve it. All of it. This is my kamma.

That's not what I meant. It's okay to suffer. You can't avoid it, but not like this. You know where it ends.

I'm not pushing it away. I embrace it. I deserve it.

That's just as bad.

What am I supposed to do? I don't have the energy to fight it. But it'll consume me.

Then stop. Do nothing.

I can't. If I do nothing, it'll take over and I'll lose my mind. And then what about him? What about his kamma?

He's only producing more suffering. For himself. For me. Where's the balance? Surely there has to be a point where the scales balance and my debt is paid for what I put him through? I'll suffer it, whatever comes my way, just tell me it'll end.

It ends when you stop suffering. Your pain fuels him.

But how do I stop it?

You don't.

That doesn't make any fucking sense. What the fuck am I thinking? I'm delirious. Need to sleep. My mind's splintering under the pressure, but my body's still buzzing like it wants to move. Escape. But there's no way to escape. You know that.

The light's so bright. Even with my eyes closed, it shines through. A glowing darkness, suggestion of orange. Red. The blood in my eyelids. Tinnitic ringing in the silence, faint voices, screaming to themselves in lonely chambers. The long echo of the music. Residual burn-in like staring at the sun too long and closing your eyes. Gone but still here, still here. Can't escape me just yet.

How do I know there aren't other rooms below mine? In adjacent houses? Pan out: an infinite matrix of tortured souls, like the proverbial Indra's net, each screaming in some vague hope that at least some faraway God might know their pain.

Good try. But you can't fool yourself. You're alone in this. You've always been alone.

Eyes blink at me. Eyes that aren't there.

Check the room to make sure. But the light's so bright. Obscures the details of the room. Amplifies my headache and nausea.

The darkness is better. A hand covers my eyes to make it all the darker. Cool fingers.

But in the not-darkness, the various pains have no body to latch onto. They drift around, collide, compete for dominance. Shoulder pain on top, now back pain from the hard ground, now stomach pain. Now the nauseous, dizzying ringing. Gradually coalescing, drifting apart, violently splitting, fading into obscurity.

It's not real. Look at you, look at how caught up you get in it all. But none of it's real.

The hammer was real.

You don't know shit, man. You'll keep on suffering until you can see through it. On and on and on. Samsara, Sam. You should know.

I see it. I know what it is. Just changing appearances in the mind. And me the detached witness. But it doesn't change the pain itself. I can't get away from it.

A sharp pain in my spine, tracing from my shoulders down to the small of my back. I arch my back, groaning.

Right here, Sam. How about that?

Grit my teeth, but the pain just builds in my head.

Suggested grins belonging to the same eyes. Always watching. They enjoy it. The only reason I'm here. Some kind of cosmic barbarity all for the entertainment of consciousness. Medieval crowds gathered to watch the latest heathen flayed or broken on the wheel. A pre-psychopathic child crushing a baby bird in its little hand, smiling a private smile at its distress. A junkie sliding the needle into his last working vein and pushing the plunger, a dirty shot that might just kill him. Part of him wishing it would. Human eyes watching it all.

Animals saw it before. Gods before that.

You like it. You want to suffer. You do it to yourself.

The hand scratches at my arm. Making for the elbow. Must be fractured. It hurts too much.

How do you know your arm hurts? Can you see it?

I know. I feel it.

I. I. I. Do you see yourself? Tell me, what do you feel?

Okay, fine, I wouldn't know it was my arm without the conditioned visual input, but I'd still feel the pain out there. My neurons would still light up.

Out where? Are you so sure?

I feel the pain. I know that much. You wouldn't know.

I wouldn't? I'll show you pain. I am pain.

Static sharpens in the darkness.

Glitter motes blinking in strobes. Gradually drifting down. But always more coming. Somewhere, a fire burning. I smell it. Is that from the house? Not a pleasant burning. My back numb and buzzing. Echoes fading out at the peripheries. Everything blurring into the now. Sleep's stolen dramas imposing themselves. You had your chance to sleep. I want to, I know I need to, but I just can't.

It's okay. It'll take what it needs.

Or is it more than sleep?

Drink it all.

He put something in the water, didn't he? Nothing I've drank since I woke here has been pure. No wonder I'm losing my mind. What, is it amphetamines to keep me awake? LSD dissolved in it? Karma's a bitch. Or maybe the dissociation and hallucinations are just the sleep deprivation. I've seen people up for a week with no sleep lost in their own minds. It all feels like drugs. It all takes you to the same place.

He was just here. Must have been five minutes. Smoked two cigarettes. The room still remembers his presence. The smoke in the stale air.

He could still be here. Sitting at the bottom of the stairs behind the door. Or watching on a hidden webcam. No hiding in the light. If you sleep, you could go too deep. He could sneak in and beat you again, cut your throat.

Deeper layers of hell lurking. Even turning the speakers back on would break me. Please don't remember. That's all I ask.

He won't come for a while. He calmed down after the beating, spaced out a bit. Unless he's already up there drinking and getting worked up, it'll be okay to sleep for a bit.

Try meditating.

Watch the breath. Let things flow. Electrical jolt up my spine. I'm not comfy.

You're never gonna be comfy.

Roll onto my good arm. Better but still pain. There's always pain. Let it be.

The breath, Sam.

Inhale. Exhale. Pain. Inhale. Exhale. Inhale. Pain. Screaming. Old woman. It came from the house. No, it didn't. What if there are others?

Exhale.

Roll over.

Open my eyes. Awareness sharpens. No going back now.

That was crazy. Vivid withdrawal dreams. Vengeful sleep taking back what was deprived for so long. Always some threat or distress. And out of this world.

Covered in sweat, even though it's cool in the room.

I check my phone. Nothing noteworthy. Pull on a t-shirt, joggers, and hoody. Light a cigarette.

The day already half gone, stretching amorphously before me. Nothing I need to do. Not so long ago, I would have killed for days off like this, but now, not so much. You always want what you don't have, always tricking yourself into thinking something else is better. Just be in the moment. Well fuck that. Not now. Need to get some food. Take a shower. Maybe smoke a bit. Not enough to get out of my head but just to help the day along.

And then what?

We'll see to that later.

My bong looks at me from my desk.

Fuck it, I'll smoke first. Why not?

Put a chill playlist on my laptop and prepare the bong. Take a good rip and exhale into the corner. Obscure Alex Grey's meditating man. Been a while since I've meditated. I should. I really should. It's probably the only thing that'll help me through this time. But every time I sit and close my eyes, she's there with me. Maybe later. I'll sit for half an hour. Once I've taken care of other shit.

The chillhop beat drags lazily behind the count. Like the passage of time doesn't bother it. Like the grave isn't racing closer in each moment.

That's why we get high.

I use my knife to disturb the weed-ash mix in the bowl and take another hit. Slide back in my chair.

That's better.

Close my eyes for a second.

The song ends, and a metal track replaces it. All blast beats and death growls. Not the vibe. Not now.

I try to skip the song, but it doesn't work. The cursor moves, but it won't click. Can't quit Spotify either. Piece of shit. I shut the laptop, but that doesn't help. Hold the off button to kill the laptop, but the music only gets louder. Fuck's sake. I stash the laptop under my pillow, but it's still screaming. Got me all worked up and anxious now.

Forget it.

I head to the kitchen, the music following me halfway down the stairs.

He's sitting at the table, staring down at his cold coffee. Cigarette smouldering in his fingers, half of it accumulated ash about to fall. He doesn't even acknowledge my presence.

I clear my throat, but he only gives me a stoned glance.

Fine, fuck you then.

I set the kettle to boil.

Still just staring blankly. What's his problem?

I prep the French press and fill it when the kettle finishes. Faint screaming. Is that? - The music's still playing. Probably keep at it until it dies. Piece of shit.

'You want a fresh coffee, mate?'

He slowly looks up at me, as though fighting a heroin high. Brown bags and waxen skin. Looks twenty years older than his age. He shrugs, nods, like it takes all his effort and concentration.

'Alright.'

I pour two cups, set his down in front of him.

He flinches. Maybe he really is high.

'Are you okay, man?'

His eyes narrow as he regards me, a hint of anger.

Like it's my fucking fault. Fine, whatever, man.

I take his old coffee and pour the dregs down the sink.

'There was so much blood.'

'What?'

I turn quickly and he shrinks back in his chair, raises his hands defensively.

'Hey man, I'm not gonna hurt you. But you want to tell me what happened?'

He shakes his head to himself. Scratches at his arm like a junky. 'You've done enough. Please. Just leave me alone. Don't hurt me again.'

'Hurt you? I didn't... fine. Just relax man.' He's in my house, but whatever. I take my coffee and head out, leaving him mumbling into his coffee.

The music's finally stopped. Thank God. My laptop probably ran out of battery. Open my door and nearly drop my coffee.

She's lying on my bed, facing the window.

'Hey.'

Close the door behind me and set my coffee down. She doesn't respond. She sleeping?

'Mina?'

I move around the bed to see her face. Her eyes are open, but they don't track me. Just staring vacantly. Her skin's pale and loose on her face, tinged with blue and purple in patches. The colour of her vibrant hippy dress continuing on her skin. Acrid smell. Dust motes glowing in the sunlight.

No. She can't be dead. Can't be right.

I lean over her, touch the back of my hand to her cold cheek. Her face yields and doesn't spring back. Print of my fingers in her mushy skin. I shouldn't have done that. Left my mark on her.

People will ask questions. They'll suspect me. Need to

get rid of the evidence. Quick.

But where? Where do I hide a body around here? A forest? River? It'd be easy if I had a car, just throw her in the boot and drive out to the middle of nowhere, but that's not an option.

I pace from the door to the bed.

Come on, Mina. You can't do this to me. Why here and now? Stop playing with me. Sit up and tear off the prosthetics. We'll both have a big laugh about it.

Joke's over.

Need a plan, and a good one. Think, man. Think.

Fuckfuckfuck.

Calm down, Sam. Breathe. Just breathe. Breathe and think.

I need to get it out of here. Need to disguise it as something else. It can't look like a body. Get her in a big box or something. Don't have anything big enough. She wouldn't fit in the big suitcase. Not unless I cut her limbs off.

Fucking barbaric. You'd do that to her?

Do I have a choice?

She wouldn't fit in my guitar case either. What about a double bass case? Probably couldn't fit her in whole even then. Maybe a big gear case. A kick drum case. Big sturdy hardware box. They'll have ones big enough. I'll buy one from a drum shop in central, bring it back in a taxi. Then, take her someplace safe.

Okay, good. Good, thinking. We'll figure the rest out later.

Need to hide her for now. Can't just leave her on my bed. In case Mum comes in. Or him.

The closet.

I take a big breath, then get one hand under her neck, one under her legs, like a big, long baby, carry her to the wardrobe, hook the door open.

Another body inside. An old rotting woman, skulking waxen face hanging from the bones. From the surprise and

107

the weight of Mina's body, I drop her, try to catch her before she hits the ground with two thuds: her feet, then louder, her head. With the closet door open, the woman slowly leans forward, crashes on top of me, sandwiching me between all the soft, rotting flesh. I shove the bitch off me and she slumps over. Her head rolls away and hits the bedroom door.

So much noise. If anyone came in now, it'd all be over.

I sit on the floor, waiting, breathing heavily inhale-exhale-inhale-exhale. I'm fucking exhausted. The room getting cloudy, the stink intoxicating me.

I retreat to the bed, tear off the duvet, stained with the faded imprint of Mina's body, and throw it over the two bodies. Still the head by the door, its cold eyes staring out at nothing.

I open the window, lean out to get some air before I pass out, rummage in my pockets for my cigarettes and lighter. Suck desperately on the cigarette. That's not gonna help. I don't care. Just need to calm myself down a minute so I can think straight and then deal with this shit. How did the old woman even get there?

You put her there. Don't you remember?

A vague memory, but I don't want to go there now. There might be no coming back.

Inhale. Exhale. Inhale.

Need to get rid of them both. Two trips with the drum case. Put them under the ground or deep at the bottom of a lake. And then I'll take so many drugs, I'll forget it all. Forget who I am.

Close my eyes, feel the breeze on my face.

Inhale. Exhale.

Inhale.

I'm going to die here. In this hole. Chained to this wall.

Maybe in death you'll escape.

Not gonna find any other way out.

But what if it's just nothingness? What if awareness itself

dies with the brain? And all those out of body experiences have only ever been produced by the brain and all of that dies with the body?

Then it'll be reborn. Over and over again. Like the stars dying and being born in far galaxies. Reborn as people from all corners of the globe and as animals, dogs and horses and rats and insects that live only a few days and as plants and lakes and mountains and the air itself and sunlight and everything at once and all the death and sickness of species, the slow burning of planets, and the still darkness going on for lifetimes.

But not me. Not just me as I am now. I don't want to be it all. I just want to be me. The life I should have had. A real life with meaning. With family and love and sunlight and rain and normal human suffering.

It's okay, Sam. It's really not so bad. It's just like waking up from a dream. You know what that feels like. But the dream's just the craziest thing. And for what it's worth, since none of it really matters in the end, it was nice to share this time with you.

It wasn't enough.

Is it ever?

Some have it better than others. Some get to grow old with the people they love.

Until they come to loathe each other? And anyway, when you die, you'll be them just as much as you are you. You're still thinking from your mortal mind.

At least you got to go quickly.

No thanks to you. It's rarely pleasant. But you get more time.

That's not a good thing. I want it to end soon. Now.

How can time be a bad thing?

Easy for you to say. You're not down here with me.

Aren't I?

Fuck. What am I doing to myself?

Whatever you need to.

I know you're not real.

None of it's real. I'm as real as you are.

Losing my mind. All the acid. No sleep.

Can you sleep while you're awake? You can wake while you sleep. What's the difference when it's so close?

God creates it all. All in the mind. What is God but a projection of the mind?

I'm not sleeping. I'm just thinking. The hum of bodily aches and pains going on beneath it, the bassline of a discordant harmony.

Come back to the room if you're not going to sleep. Ground yourself and you won't get lost so much.

Creeping in on my periphery. The light is so bright, my vision can't process it all. Black blotchy glaucoma. But the room's covered in insects. The walls and the ceiling. Closing in on me. Ears ringing with their collective buzzing. The fear shocks my nervous system into fuzzy overdrive. They're not real. That's why they can't reach you. You can't touch them. Just my mind playing tricks.

The shit still stinks. It goes straight to my stomach and bucks a few times but nothing comes up. Sit up, my whole spine bending and straightening like an old copper pipe. How old people must feel.

See, you get to experience your old age after all. You get to shit yourself and lose your marbles and watch your body fall apart.

Be here. Stay with awareness. Awareness is never wrong, never insufficient.

Hold my hands in my lap.

Inhale.

Exhale.

Just this. Nothing more.

A few of the insects fall away but never land.

In your mind. All in your mind.

My left eye twitches. Pain hums to itself. My arse stinging where I haven't been able to wipe properly.

The whole room bleached like an old film. Vision still blotchy but faintly red now. Maybe there's something wrong with my eyes. Bleeding inside?

And nothing I can do about it.

I rub my left eye. When I open it again, the blotches are just as many, but they've moved across the room.

I'm a fucking mess. Every inch of me.

All because of this room. Because of him. I'm going to die here, and conditions are only going to get worse before then.

So much worse. You can't imagine it. You think it's bad now.

If Mum could see me now. It'd break her. She'd never sleep again.

I miss you so much. I took you for granted. Should have hugged you more. Called more when I was away. Told you I loved you. I was so lost in my own world. I never knew how precious the time was.

Vision blurs more, a frosted film behind which sepia light flickers, shapes blend and break apart, suggestions of so many things that are and aren't there.

I'm sorry.

If only you were happy. But how can you be when your son is missing? Hoping for the best but dreading the worst, knowing with each passing day, each week that something's really wrong.

And all for what? A few grand buried in the garden she'll never find. She deserved a good, loving son. I was supposed to take care of her in her old age. And instead she got me. And now not even that.

Shaking. Deep leg aches, too warm and buzzing, feel the blood, but I stay cross-legged. Take a deep breath. Close my eyes.

Sensation of plunging down a dark hole. Furtherfurtherfurtherfurther. Then white light, an endless expanse of space behind my eyelids and impossible constellations flickering in the distance. Whispers in alien language.

Don't. Forget these empty phenomena. What is really

here?

Inhale. Exhale.

Maternal sorrow. So much pain because of you.

But Mum will be okay. Eventually. Over the years and the decades, her wounds will heal. One day she'd even forget your face without photographs. Forget your voice. She'll throw out your things. Repurpose your room. When you're long dead, she will live on, doing just fine without you dragging her down.

I just want her to be at peace. Please, let her be at peace. She deserves that much.

Inhale.

Exhale.

May you be at peace.

Inhale.

May you be happy.

Exhale.

Inhale.

I'm sorry.

May you be free from suffering.

Everyone suffers.

Free from unnecessary suffering. Be at peace with the aches and the pains.

Like you?

May you be at peace.

And what about Mina's mum?

I'd wish her the same if she were still living.

And what about him?

He doesn't want to be happy. Doesn't want to be at peace.

Doesn't he? Doesn't he deserve love? Karunā?

He wouldn't accept it. He knows only hate. He's blinded by it.

Have you offered it?

How am I supposed to show compassion?

He hurt you. Every day he makes you suffer.

I have no agency here. I couldn't show him love if I

112

wanted to.

If. If. If.

You hate him. You want him to suffer like you've suffered. Kamma. Samsara. It's only right. And round and round it goes. Hate fuelling hate. Suffering fuelling suffering.

You'd kill him if he only gave you the chance.

You'd be right to.

Can't you love that which you kill? Kill what you love?

You'd do the same if you were in his position. If you felt what he feels. If you'd lived every minute of his life like he has.

He is you. Just like you're every being and being itself.

There is love for him then. As there is love for all the universe.

Yes, but you don't really feel it.

How can I? How can you ask me to?

How can you expect to be free from suffering? You know the cause of dukkha. You've seen it. And you know the end of dukkha. You've seen it too. A thousand times over.

I wish him peace.

Inhale. Exhale.

May you be at peace.

And mean it.

His silhouette towering over me. The heat of his hatred reaching me in waves.

May you be happy.

Why?

You really think if he finds peace, he'll let you go? He'll never let you go. It'd be a death sentence. You'd go to the police.

I wouldn't.

He could never know that. You'll die here, whether he's at peace or caught up in animal rage.

It doesn't matter.

I'll suffer no matter what. His suffering doesn't negate

mine. His suffering brings me nothing.

May you be free from suffering.

Sitting there, staring down at the floor. Smoke rising from his cigarette.

I'm sorry. I forgive you.

May you be at peace.

You're wasting your fucking time. Lying to yourself.

Inhale. Achingachingaching. Head throbbing. There was so much blood. Exhale. Eye twitching even when they're closed. Body moaning. Just let us die. Are you gonna try and blow it out, love? Inhale.

May you be happy.

Fuck him. Kill him first chance you get. It's the only way and you know it.

May you be at peace.

Footsteps coming down the steps.

Coming back. He's coming back. Whatever happens, just be calm. Be this open space, this boundless compassion. Give his anger and hatred nowhere to land.

The lock clicks and the door opens. He comes awkwardly into the room carrying a Sainsbury's bag and a red blanket slung over his shoulder.

For me? Please let it be for me.

He leaves the door ajar, walks to the edge of my reach and lowers to his haunches. Like I'm a vicious dog that might pull against my chain and go for him at any second. From the bag he takes a tin of baked beans. No, beans with sausages. Sets it on the ground. A bottle of water too.

Oh God, thank God.

He drops the blanket on the floor.

I meet his eyes. Try to show gratitude. 'Thank you.'

'Mm. And clean your shit up.' He nods to the corner and pushes the bag towards me. Inside are kitchen roll and antibacterial spray.

'Thanks.'

He straightens up and heads out.

My heart's thundering in my chest. Is this real? I'm not hallucinating this? Pinch my arm. Both arms.

I crawl forward, throw the blanket around my shoulders and tuck the bottom underneath me. The warmth and softness like a maternal hug. Safety. I tear the top off the tin. Like Christmas haha. Claw the food into my mouth with two fingers. Meaty and salty and almost a little sweet. My mouth lights up and my stomach moans in ecstasy as the food goes down. I've never known such pleasure and comfort from food. And to think it comes from a shitty tin of cold beans and sausage.

I laugh as I take another mouthful, wash it down with a little water. More ecstasy. Like water from the first spring, wetting my mouth and throat for the first time. I don't even care if he has spiked it. I hope he has. Of all the drugs I've taken and all the crazy shit I've experienced, who would have thought this here would rival it all? Sitting in a cold, shitty basement tripping out my fucking mind. I almost spit the water out from laughing. Back to the food. Maybe next time he'll bring me a full English. Caviar with a glass of his finest red wine. The walls laugh with me.

Should save some for later. Already less than half left. I set the tin by the wall, wipe my fingers and mouth with a square of kitchen roll. Shuffle back to the wall, lean my head against my shoulder, rubbing my cheek on the soft fabric.

Fucking luxury man. Arab princes haven't had it this good. Haha. Hahaha. Losing my fucking mind. But it's fine. Compared to a few hours ago, I'm in fucking paradise.

Getting stiff already half-against the wall. Bloody cuff.

I curl up on the ground, get the blanket between me and the cold tiles. Close my eyes. Snug us a bug haha. Food in my belly. Yeah, this isn't bad.

Why the change of heart? Was it the mettā? Did my mantras have some mystical effect on him?

It doesn't work like that.

But what if it does? What if I've been wrong about materiality this whole time? What if I am more God than I am man and I can manifest compassion in the world, move other people to goodness through sheer intention? If I did it for hours, days on end, maybe he would let me out.

Don't fucking kid yourself. You really are insane.

Maybe there is a God closer to the Abrahamic one than the ground of being in the East.

Please, help me. You have the power to save me. I'll be good. I'll live my life in service to you.

If there's a God that can do anything to alleviate your suffering, it's the very same God that put you in this shithole to start with. Don't be making deals with that motherfucker.

No. It probably had nothing to do with the mettā. Just a coincidence. He probably just felt guilty after beating me with the hammer.

The food and water's only keeping you alive to suffer longer. If he really had mercy, he'd have killed you already. Quick knife across the throat and blood running over the tiles. Or better still, pipe some carbon monoxide into the basement and gas me out.

But the blanket. He didn't need to do that.

Maybe there is some good in him after all. A truly evil man, a psychopath wouldn't have done that.

Maybe I can reach him. Maybe I can connect with his better nature.

What's going through his mind right now?

What if that's the end of the torture? The beatings at least. And the speakers and the fans. He hasn't turned anything back on yet.

I should sleep. My mind's still buzzing with the excitement of the treats on top of everything else. The light burning through my eyelids. Thumbs pressing them. Whole head aching. But it has to give eventually.

Come on, you know you need the sleep. Just let it happen. What's wrong with you?

Eat a bit more first. And drink some.

Piss, too. You need to piss or it'll wake you up. Don't want to piss all over your precious new blanket.

But I'm so comfy like this.

But still hungry. Half a tin of beans and processed sausage was nothing in comparison. I can smell it inches from my nose.

I pull the tin towards me, pour some food into my mouth, and lie there chewing it, breathing heavy. God, it tastes so good though. Take a second to recover, then go back for more. Until it's all gone. Then wash it down with more water. Leave about a third for later.

Need to piss now. Don't have any empty bottles. Maybe I should just drain the rest of the water so I can use the bottle.

Don't. It could be days until you get more. Better to pace yourself.

Fine.

I sit up awkwardly, draw the blanket back, and piss into the tin. The piss turns orangey as it mixes with the sauce residue lining the tin. Push it as far as I can into the corner, then settle back on the floor.

I'll need to shit too. But not just yet. Sleep first. If I can.

Fucking exhausted. And now we're safe for a bit.

Close my eyes and imagine I'm back home. No, the ground's too hard. Just my bunk at the monastery. Rich asleep next door and the night birds murmuring outside. Open skies and peaceful fields spanning miles. No place I'd rather be.

Inhale.

Exhale.

Inhale.

Exhale.

Inhale.

Exhale.

In-

Lock clicks, and metal raps on metal.

I wake too fast, heart racing ahead of me. I slept in despite the sun. Not like me.

But still feel like shit. Muscles still tense and a heavy cloak of fatigue. Couldn't get to sleep for ages. That's right. Staring at the ceiling for hours. Pacing the few steps from the door to the window and doing push ups to try to tire myself out.

Could try and sleep some more, but guys are already talking in the corridor. If I skip breakfast, I might get a little peace and quiet. But it's canteen day. At least there's that.

I drag my bones off the bunk, splash some water in my face, drink some, look for my toothbrush, but it's not by the sink. Not on my shelf, on the windowsill. What the fuck? Where did I put it? I definitely used it to brush last night. Didn't I?

The memory's hazy, obscured by the night, but I must have. I would have noticed if it was missing. But that means it must have disappeared in the night.

My heart doesn't let up. Skin getting hot.

They can't have taken it through a locked door. A screw must have snuck in when I eventually passed out and taken it. Probably make a shank with it to frame me. They don't want me to ever get out. They'll leave it lying around for someone to use in a hit, and then they'll blame me for it. Add another few years to my sentence. Pull something similar in a few years to keep me here. I'll grow old and waste away here. Muscles atrophy and skin wrinkle. Mind turn to water.

Motherfuckers.

I definitely didn't put it down somewhere. Scan the pad, check under my mattress, inside my shoes. It didn't fall down anywhere.

Don't kid yourself. You knew they took it. Always out to get me. I'm guilty in their eyes, and that's all that matters for them to do whatever they want to me.

Fucking bastards. Just wait til I get my hands on them. If I'm never getting out, I've got nothing to lose. May as well make them pay. Fucking idiots. They're turning me into a killer.

You did that yourself. You deserve everything you get.

I never asked for this shit.

Roll a cigarette with the last dust in my pouch. At least I'll get more in a couple of hours when they deliver canteen. I smoke at the window, watching the single, leafless branch of the corner tree blow into view, disappear again, playing hide and seek. Looks like it's gonna rain soon. Kind of hope it does. I wouldn't mind feeling the rain on my face during yard time. As long as it doesn't piss it down and they cancel it.

Yeah, that's a little better. But the cigarette's gone too soon. And no more until my canteen comes. They better not fuck it up or they'll have hell to pay. Wouldn't surprise me. Always playing games with me.

Maybe I should just kill myself. Take a couple screws with me. The worst ones. I'd be doing the world a favour.

See that's why you're in here. And you make out like you don't belong.

They made me this way.

You were always this way. Follow after your piece of shit dad.

Inhale. Exhale.

Getting lost. You know what that means?

Yeah yeah, I know.

Fold my blanket four ways, drop it by the bed, and sit. Feel my hands together. Drop my gaze to the floor in front of the door. See those motherfuckers coming if they try anything. I'd hear the door anyway, but I'm not taking any chances. Not with them conspiring against me. Who knows what else they're plotting.

The breath, Sam.

Deep inhale.

Deep exhale.

Aches running up and down my back.

Yelling further down the wing. The more dominant, the louder. Laughter.

Laughing at me.

The little pussy that won't come out his cell. Thinks he's too good to associate with us.

They're only bad news. Rapists and murderers. I've got my mind. A cell's not so bad when you can escape inside yourself. Those animals haven't been mindful for a second in their lives. Just following one impulse to the next without a moment's thought. Always asleep. No idea what reality really is.

You should pity them. They don't know any different.

Inhale.

Wind rages outside. Might be a storm coming. That'd be good.

Exhale.

Inhale.

What have I got coming in my canteen? Tobacco. Crisps, breakfast bars. Baked beans. Orange squash. I'll need to order a new toothbrush for next week. Have to make do without in the meantime. Let my teeth rot in my mouth.

Fucking bastards. How could they do this to me? How do they sleep at night?

Thinking. Thinking again.

Fuck. My mind's so sticky today. Must be the lack of sleep.

Still thinking.

Inhale.

Exhale.

Stay with the breath, Sam.

So tired still. Tossing and turning most of the night. Tortured by thought. Thinking of Mina. She was talking to me.

Laughter. Fucking monkeys in cages. That's all they are. All you are.

I didn't mean to kill her. And I regret what I did. Not like most of them. They don't give a fuck about anyone but themselves.

You always see the best in people.

Come on, that's not fair. You don't know what it's like

120

in here. I see good in good people. They're all just sleepwalkers. If ordinary people are asleep, these ones are another layer deep. Limbic apes locked in with each other.

That's all they are?

There is some goodness, but good is weak in here, and they'll sniff out any weakness and prey on it. The ones that'll never leave, they don't care about anything. And why should they? Most of them aren't compatible with normal society, but I am. I just made a mistake.

I know. And they made their mistakes too. You'll get out of here one way or another. You won't die in here. How could you? Come home to me. You know I'm always waiting.

What if you die first?

Don't be silly.

Takes my hand, draws me to her and I watch the world over her shoulder. Our little world. But not forever.

Come on, get out of here. You can't be here.

Why not?

You know why. He'll find out. You need to be careful, Sam. Your life depends on it.

He won't kill me.

But you're not leaving there. Not unless you act. You know how to reach him.

How?

The same way you reached me.

I can't.

You can.

I have to kill him.

Sam.

What?

You know what you need to do. You're already doing it.

Laughing. Different directions.

Open my eyes and the room's immediate again. Voices outside the door. Screw shouting. Canteens.

I get up, take a deep breath.

Inhale. Exhale. Open the door.

Everyone lining up for canteen. Only make passing eye contact. Glancing back to the screw. Like a magnet, everyone's attention on him and his goody bags.

He gets to me, hands me an orange Sainsbury's bag instead of the clear, sealed ones. I look inside. A double pack of kitchen roll, the crisps and chocolate bar I ordered, but a tin of cat food. Another one in the bottom.

What's this about?

What, you got something to say?

This is wrong. This isn't what I wanted.

You think I give a fuck? You get what's given to you and you should be thanking us on your knees cause if it were up to me, you wouldn't get shit.

I check the bag again on the way back to my pad. Just fucking with me. Trying to make me lose my mind. Trying to make me suffer.

Pace the cell but my foot starts to ache. I lie down but the pain's so bad, it makes everything go white, and then there's nothing for a bit, and then the pain's here again. But the soft blanket on my skin too. The gentle touch.

It's okay, Sam.

Stomach ringing like a church bell. I look for the can, but I finished it. Full of piss in the corner. Can't you smell it?

When will I get more? I need more. And the water's low. Throat's sore so I drink a little.

Need to shit.

Hate it. Hate having this body and its gruelling demands.

Who's punishing who?

It's him. It's all him.

Is it? Remember mettā.

There was a connection.

A brief liberation.

I had it for a moment.

Am I finally experiencing it? The breakthrough. Enlightenment sustaining itself, not merely a passing glimpse.

Drag myself to my knees, crawl away from the cuff.

That's not enlightenment.

Stand to shit. Already coming. The stink of old mess wafting up from the corner.

At least I have the kitchen roll.

It felt like nibbāna. I know what it feels like.

Yes, but you trick yourself too. How do you really know? Maybe you just thought you were enlightened, but the enlightenment itself was just an object of thought and you lost in it.

What's the difference?

There is enlightenment, but you are not enlightened.

That doesn't make sense. I'm everything.

The shit slaps the floor, the smell already intensifying. My stomach hurts as the second lot comes, wetter than the first. Some infection lurking up in my gut. Feels like something's wrong. Maybe I'm just paranoid.

That's how he wants me. Terrified at every possibility. Killers in the corners.

I wipe off, drop the papers in the bag, then fold a new stretch and pick up my own shit. Spray the ground and wipe the residue up. Clean my hands off again. Still feel some residue but the kitchen towel will never totally get rid of it. Could use some of the water.

No. We don't have water to waste.

What am I supposed to do about the can of piss? Can't throw it away. Forget it. I can't reach the bottle, so I toss the shitty bag away and crawl back to the blanket.

That's better. The safety of the blanket. Already filthy with the outline of my body. Bloody patches and yellow stains.

I really don't look good. Even after the food, you can see my ribs clearly through the skin. My own being siphoned off just to keep me alive.

You are not this body. The wounds and wasting only tell a history of this flesh and blood. A painting. You think this is you?

I know. I'm everything. But everything includes this human form. The one I have to feel every second of every day. The one I have to die with.

Back to the blanket. That's better. Hide the damage. Hide the truth. Close my eyes. Can't see my body. How do I know it's really there?

The pain. The pain tells me where it is. But it's only a memory of the body that locates the pain. Given time, I'd forget where the body really should be and the pains and aches would bleed out across the sensory stratosphere.

It's all just conditioning. You suffer because you've conditioned yourself to suffer.

I didn't do it. They did that.

You played your part.

Yes, but I'm done with that. I know my sins. I want to move towards the light. What else can I do?

The light? How's that going for you? Open your eyes and you'll see the light.

Stomach groans. The softly burning weight down there somewhere. Touch my hand against it with the small comfort it offers.

It's just hunger, Sam. You're starving to death.

He has to bring more food soon. I'll beg him.

He just gave it to you. Judging by the pattern, it'll be another few days, whatever that means at this point.

I'll die before I get a chance to make a move.

A glimmer of mercy from him, but it's not enough. He doesn't know what he's doing to me. He doesn't know how close I'm getting.

He doesn't care.

Maybe he would, if he knew. Or maybe he'll get pissed off and waterboard me some day with cans of beer.

Nothing I can do.

Need to meditate. Repeat the mettā.

Drop back. Look for the breath. Follow it.

Inhale. Exhale.

But I'm so dizzy. It's worse when I meditate. In the

confusion of thought, it gets lost.

Stay with it. Watch it.

I can't bear it.

So avoid it. Push it away. See where that goes.

I know. I know. There's no need to be like that.

Inhale.

Exhale.

Try to picture him. No, don't start with him.

Mum. Picture her calm. In peaceful meditation herself. Or smiling. Imagine her laughing. But I can't. Can barely see her face. Even in a photograph.

Can't even remember my mum's face. It's there, it's deep in there, but my access is shut off. You don't deserve to think of her.

It's okay. You don't need to see her. Just invoke her. Wish her happiness.

May you be happy.

Despite everything.

You never deserved a son like me. All the pain I've caused you.

Getting lost again. Stay with it.

Slow, wavering breathing.

May you be happy.

May you be at peace.

How well did you know her?

Mina?

He nods.

We were friends, I guess. For a few months.

Not her dealer?

A smirk in his voice.

For a little while. I'd say we were friends too.

Mm. You knew her through Ella?

Yeah.

What did you sell her?

Weed mostly. Molly and coke a handful of times.

And that's what killed her.

Yeah.

Nods again. Hard stare. Holding it in. But at any moment he could break.

You cut it?

Inhale. Exhale.

Only with caffeine and detergent powder.

Detergent?

Like I normally did. There was something else in it. One of my suppliers must have put something nasty in it. Fentanyl probably.

So it's someone else's fault.

I mean, I sold them to her. That was wrong. But someone else cut it, knowing the danger.

He just blinks.

I should just kill you. It'd only be right. A life for a life. Two lives.

I nod slowly.

What's wrong with you?

Maybe you're right.

You want me to kill you? Yeah, you want an easy way out. But you don't deserve a quick death.

I nod again. I know.

Why are you so fucking calm?

I've stopped fighting it. There's no me to fear death or suffering. And I understand it. I understand what I did to you and that nothing I do or say is going to change what you do now. So I'm at peace with it.

No no no. You don't get to be at peace.

He gets up and looks to hit me or kick me, but doesn't.

You can be at peace too.

Shut up with your Buddhist bullshit. You don't know what I feel. Every fucking day.

I know suffering. As deep as you fall into it.

He stares, trying to place me. Lights a cigarette and sits in the chair.

Life is suffering. That's something you lot say, isn't it?

In a way.

So tell me. Tell me how you can go through all the shit you've been through and sit there so fucking calm?

I found enlightenment. Turns out suffering is an easy primer.

You're welcome. So what, I'm supposed to let you torture me now and I'll forget all my troubles and become a Buddha myself?

No. But I can help you. It'd be the least I could do.

How?

I can guide you away from suffering.

With all your Buddhist philosophy?

Freedom from suffering is a central teaching, but it doesn't have to be in Buddhist language. The language doesn't matter. It's the true nature of reality that counts.

He starts pacing. Doesn't look at me.

You know what I think? I think you've lost your mind.

Would that be such a bad thing? Maybe we need to lose our mind to find it.

He pauses, smiles to himself, and flicks his cigarette end into the corner.

Goodnight, Sam.

He heads out, killing the light on his way.

The boy checks over his shoulder one final time, then goes in his mother's handbag, finds her green Rizlas, tears out one, two, three, four, five. That'll do. Puts them carefully in his pocket. A stick of filters from the box. Two. She won't notice. Opens her tobacco pouch and tears off a big scraggly lump of it, holds it in his fist like a spider he's caught, and carries it back to his room. Releases the tobacco onto his desktop and tries to roll a cigarette the way he's watched Mum and Dad do a hundred times. But it's harder with your own fingers. The paper and the tobacco work against your fingertips, refuse your will. Eventually he gets it into a shabby uneven rollie. Takes the lighter hidden in his top drawer, goes to the window, opens it, lights the cigarette. Draws on it. Holds the cough in. Only pussies cough.

Exhales slowly out the window. Watches the smoke drift out and get caught in a breeze that carries away any trace of it.

He hits it again, holding it between his thumb and index finger like he's seen in movies sometimes. Not like his parents hold it between two fingers. Just to try it. He won't get addicted like them. He won't get angry without it like his dad. Already feeling the extra blood in his forehead. The hazy feeling. A little faint but not unpleasant.

He draws the smoke into his lungs, watching Mr Harrison step out of his back door and go into their shed. Exhales. Feeling kind of bad for a second. Shame. Not about the cigarette but about the need for it. The growing tension in his viscera. But that too dissipates, just as quickly as the smoke in the breeze.

May you be happy.

Sitting on the curb. Raises the bottle to his lips and drinks deep. Forget her. She's not worth your time. You can't trust other people. Not family, not friends, most of all not girls.

Figures spill out from the doorway and linger on the pavement, looking around and talking. One of them looks his way.

He gets up and heads down the road. Takes another swig from his bottle. And another to empty it. Walks a few steps, glances over his shoulder. They haven't followed him yet. Some good distance between them. He hurls the bottle at a brick wall and it shatters, fragments bouncing back across the pavement. He doesn't feel any better about it. Just a tinge of shame.

May you be at peace.

He cuts the rails up with expert precision, separating the powder into three equal parts, shaping them into lines, collecting any residue, reshaping the lines. Puts the half-straw up his nostril and hoovers the first line. Blood rushes to the brain. Skin tingles. Thoughts quicken. Everything flowing now. He switches nostrils and cleans up the second line.

Keeps sniffing like he's trying to catch a scent. Swills his mouth with beer and swallows it. Keeps swallowing to move the drip along. The pain already forgotten. Everything clear and bright and vivid. Itching to do something, fingers busy themselves by lighting a smoke.

May you be free from suffering.

The sudden stillness wakes me. Dark outside the windows. No sign of a platform. We can't be here yet.

Other passengers rousing from sleep, abandoning books and tablets, looking around for explanation.

Probably just a signalling issue. Waiting for a light. I close my eyes and lean against the window.

A woman's cry opens my eyes. The lights flicker in the carriage ceiling. She awkwardly laughs off her surprise, a hand against her chest. But then distressed voices from far ahead of us. The next carriage.

Something's happened.

The tannoy crackles, a faint voice muttering. I strain to hear but can't make out words. He's not talking to us but trying to console himself.

The lights cut out, leaving the carriage in darkness, but there's light still flickering ahead in the next carriage. I get up and feel my way down the aisle to the vestibule door. The button to open it doesn't work, but I hit the outer door button and the door slides slowly back a few inches, then stops. I pull it open the rest of the way and climb down into the cold, dark tunnel.

Need to get somewhere safe.

Nowhere's safe.

Safer than here.

I reach up and try the door for the next carriage. It slowly draws back with a high-pitched screech. I climb up, back to the stuffy warmth of the train. Head down the aisle to the next carriage where the light's stable.

The guy on the tannoy sobbing to himself over the static.

Please. Not like this. Please please please.

Passengers glance at me as I walk past the constant fluctuating light-dark-light-dark-light.

A mother hugging her two young children to her chest. Regarding me as some passing harbinger of the hell to come.

An old couple sleeping. Or maybe dead.

Gone-here-gone-here-gone.

Teenage boy looks up from his games console, headphones over his ears. Looks annoyed at me like all of this is my fault.

Gone-here-gone-here.

Buddhist monk in pumpkin-orange garb sat cross-legged on the double seat. Eyes closed and a faint smile on his face.

He knows.

Gone-here-gone-here-gone-here.

An arm stretched out in a shoelace tourniquet. Gone-here-gone. He slides the needle into his vein, pushes the plunger. Here-gone-here. His head falls back and he regards me with sad resignation.

Good while it lasted.

Gone-here-gone-here-gone-here.

Keep going. Get to the light. But it flashes out.

Keep moving. Just keep moving.

Feeling along the seats. A hand grabs mine.

Please. Help me.

I can't even help myself. I'll come back if I can.

I shake the hand off, keep moving. Feeling out in front of me and eventually hit the door. Feel the button. Get my fingers between the vestibule doors and pull them open.

A breeze hits me. Whistling down the tunnel.

There is no next coach. No cab and no driver.

Only the tunnel stretching on and on with no glimpse of light. But I have to keep going.

Climb down from the coach and walk on the tracks, both hands out in front of me and pinning my ears for any sounds of movement.

Keep walking keep walking keep walking keep walking keep walking keep walking keep walking keep walking keep walking keep walking getting exhausted. My legs heavy and numb. Can't go on much longer but I have to. Have to keep walking keep walking keep walking. I plant my foot but when I shift my weight, it buckles. I hit the ground and lie there breathing heavy with my cheek on the cold rail. Just lie here. You'll die here. I don't have a choice. At least I can rest a moment. Be with myself. Be with awareness.

Hey. Sam.

No. Let me sleep.

Body here on the ground but floating slightly above it too. Ignore the aches and the contact. Stay with awareness. Sensation blurring. Second body rising. Gentle movement of air on skin. Second breath inhaling, exhaling.

Sam.

It's gone. Just me and my body here on the basement floor with my everyday aches and pains. My throbbing head.

What the fuck do you want?

Light at the window. Barely. Moonlight illuminating only the corner. A dash of orange. The Sainsbury's bag.

A face shifts at the window. Eyes staring down at me.

I sit up, heart beating hard.

How did you get there?

Jesus, what's he done to you?

It's okay. It was worse. With a little luck, it'll improve more. I just need some more food. Medicine. Some good sleep. I could sleep for days without waking.

You need to get out of there man.

I jerk my ankle back against the cuff. The hot sting triggers a sickening jolt in my stomach.

I can't. If I could get out of here, don't you think I would have by now?

Small, pale fingers grip the window bars and the face presses into the gap.

131

It's not real. The chain's only as real as you want it to be.

Bullshit. I don't want it to be real. I want to get up and walk out of here. You need to help me. Bring help. Please.

You know I can't do that. You're on your own.

Well, fuck you then. You're just as bad as him, watching me suffer.

The face retreats, fingers peel off the bars.

No, wait, I'm sorry. Come back.

But the light dissolves with the face. I try to blink back the light, but there's only darkness, buzzing with static.

There is no window. You know this. You're on your own. Losing my fucking mind. Won't even let me sleep.

You do it to yourself.

Rage burns in me. The urge to hit out, to scream. To use my energy for something. But there's nothing I can do. Pull at my ankle cuff, the pain flares, keep tugging, gritting my teeth. Getting nowhere but at least the pain is something. Some release. Ankle cold. No, wet. Touch it with my fingers. Bleeding again.

Look what you've done. Just making things worse for yourself.

He was right.

You do it to yourself. Again and again and again. Endless cycle of samsara and dukkha.

Thought you were over this.

When's it going to end?

Touch my burning ankle again. I'm sorry. Wipe the blood on the bottom of the blanket. Press my cheek against the softness. Arms into my chest.

Pathetic. Look at you. Like a fucking baby.

Just thoughts. Empty. Where are they now? See how insubstantial they are. But you become so easily identified with them. You become them.

Aches in my whole body in their absence. The panic always nesting in my gut.

Always?

Watch the impermanence. Anicca. Remember your

teachings, Sam. You've been here before. A thousand times. Don't get caught up.

Drop back. Watch the breath.

Watching. Inhale. Exhale. But who's watching that? Me. Watching over my own shoulder.

Who is watching? You?

There is no watcher. All this suffering and no real witness.

You still don't get it.

I do. I know. I just forget. It draws me back in.

It's okay. It does that.

I've seen the truth. So clearly I think I could never forget. But then I do.

But it's getting better. Yes. Enlightenment right here, then gone the next, then here again.

Gone? Where does it go? Where could it possibly go?

No. That's right. It's always here, whether I'm aware of it or not. That's the point. That's the point.

Getting caught up in thoughts of enlightenment or non-enlightenment, that's just missing the mark again.

Forget about it. This is it right here.

I just have to show him. If he only knew what I know.

He will see. He wants the suffering to end. He's starting to see it. If you show him the way, he will follow.

And maybe then -

Don't.

It might be my only way out.

Don't do it to yourself.

Maybe then he'll free me. I can live again. I can go home and hug Mum and spend my days with the sangha and serve them, serve the world. I'll never so much as swat a fly. I'll let any insect crawl on me and be at home. I won't lust for anything. With my eyes wide open, I'll live my life like a lucid dream, holding the truth in each moment and shining the light of it on every person I meet. A bodhisattva among them. And all this suffering will make sense. It'll be worth it because I stared dukkha in the face and saw its true nature, and only with the understanding it gave me will I lead others from the darkness. The horror becomes blessing. It will all be worth it.

I said don't.

You're never getting out of here.

Would you do it then? If easing his suffering wouldn't help you? If it even increased your own suffering? Then your enlightenment is an illusion. A trick. And you have to trick yourself to trick him.

I would. Regardless of what it means for me. Because he doesn't know. And without knowledge, his suffering will never end. This pain and madness, I can take it because I know the truth. If I have the power to ease his suffering, I'll do it. It's my nature.

He knocks, immediately opens the door, and slugs in. Lights a cigarette on his way to the chair, draws it away from the shitty corner. He looks exhausted, ill maybe. How long's it been? A couple days? If he's ill, I could catch it. It could kill me.

Maybe it's just late and he's tired, a little drunk. No idea what time it is. Could be three a.m.

He closes his eyes as he sucks on the cigarette, then stares at me through a haze, like I'm just part of the wall. Like I'm barely here.

Why is he here? Does he even know?

He looks high. Smells like beer and smoke.

So tell me.

I sit up properly. My back winces as it straightens.

Tell you what?

How to stop the pain.

Inhale. Exhale.

Well, first you have to understand it. I mean really understand it. Look deep into it without flinching.

I've been deep. You don't know how deep it goes.

The pain creeps into his voice. Wavers.

I know. I think if there's one thing we can say for sure,

it's that we've both suffered a fucking lot these past few years.

He looks up at me, not a hint of a smile, but nods.

When you look into your suffering, you can't resist it. You have to accept it exactly as it is. Otherwise you're just fighting with yourself, you're fuelling the very fire you want to put out. It sounds paradoxical, but only when you truly accept your suffering does it disappear. You realise there's nothing really there. Just smoke and mirrors. Thoughts leading to feelings leading to thoughts, round and round, a negative feedback loops that sustains itself. But nothing at centre. There's this analogy the Buddha uses of the two arrows. The first arrow, that's worldly pain. You can't avoid that. That's death and disease and physical pain and fear and all the nastiness we have to deal with as living beings. But the second arrow, that's your response to the pain. That's your mind. The fighting with the pain, always wishing it away, that's the kind of existential suffering you feel deep within you and that never seems to go away. But there's good news. Because we can dodge the second arrow. We see it coming after the first arrow and we calmly sidestep it. Once we accept whatever worldly suffering comes our way, we don't suffer it in our souls. I don't mean like a Christian soul, just a figure of speech. But we can avoid all of that suffering deep within us, and then we realise that the worldly suffering isn't really so bad and we can find peace even in its presence.

Not so bad?

I raise my hands.

I don't mean that it doesn't hurt. I know the pain my actions have caused you. I just mean that most of your suffering is created in the mind.

It's all in my head, yeah? That's what you're saying?

The drunken anger creeping back in. Come on, he must understand what I'm saying.

I mean that's how consciousness is. That's how it is for all of us, and I've experienced it myself. I do experience it that way.

Well, good for you. Yeah, you're great with your metaphors and your philosophy, but how does that actually fucking help me? What am I supposed to do with that?

That's the harder part. It's one thing to understand it all intellectually, but it's about living it. Restructuring your consciousness around this truth.

Yeah, and how do I do that?

How do we?

We meditate. And we read spiritual texts. The Buddha's words and those who understood his teachings. We let it work its way into our thoughts and our feelings. Grow from a seed into a great tree.

So I should meditate and read Buddhist scripture? That's your solution?

I guess so. But as I say, it's really about transforming your mind. The meditation and the reading aren't important themselves. They're just tools to help us see reality for what it really is.

Then what do I need you for? I can download a meditation app and buy some books online. Why don't I just put you out of your misery right now?

Inhaleexhaleinhale.

Only you can answer that question. If you think it's best, then I won't fight it. What am I going to do to stop you, anyway? But I would say, it would be a lot harder without me. It always helps to have a teacher who's been there before, who's trodden the same path you're trying to walk. It's easy to get lost and give up early on. I can guide you a lot easier than a simple app. And anyway, a lot of the popular meditation apps and books miss the point. The truth gets obscured in translation. You really need someone who's as close to the Buddha's teachings as possible.

He just sits there. Reaches for his cigarettes, but his hand slows, falls back to his leg.

Alright.

He glances back at the door.

Tomorrow, you'll teach me to meditate.

Okay. I'll show you.

He gets to his feet.

Do you think I could get some more food? And a little water? Painkillers maybe? You know, the better shape I'm in, the better I can help you.

He smirks.

Yeah, you'd fucking like that, wouldn't you?

Just watch the breath. Inhale. Exhale…Inhale… Exhale.

Only darkness behind my closed eyes. He could sneak up at any moment and grab me. A blade in my belly. Hands around my neck.

He won't. You've got him onside. For now at least.

I keep thinking. Can't concentrate on the breath.

It's okay. Don't stress about it. Don't slip into the reaction. Just let it pass. And look for it again. The breath isn't really the point. Just to focus the mind.

Silence. More silence. Why do I get the feeling he's watching me? Or planning something. Steal a look, but he's still in the chair with his eyes closed. Hands fidgeting in his lap.

You can also try counting the breaths as another tool to focus the mind. Count the inbreath and outbreath as one. In. Out. One. In. Out. Two. Just to ten. And then back to one. Although sometimes just counting ten breaths can be enough to still the mind, and then you can just let the mind flow.

Count. Don't count. What do you want me to do?

Sorry, I'm getting ahead of myself. Just count to ten. And then you can stop.

Count to ten? That's your deep philosophical insight?

No. Only a stepping stone. The counting's not the point. The breath's not the point.

So why don't you just tell me the point?

You have to see it for yourself. I can only guide you along the way. You have to see for yourself.

This is bullshit. You make out like you're all enlightened, but I know exactly what you're doing.

Trying to help you?

Trying to manipulate me. Yeah, that's what you're up to. You think if you get me all zen and sedated with your religious bullshit, I'll let you go. I'll say no worries, Sam. It's all forgiven. No hard feelings.

Glaring at me. Face red in the bright light.

No. I'm not anticipating that.

You're not anticipating it?

If you let me go, you'd never be certain I wouldn't go to the police. Although I know I wouldn't, and even if you didn't think I would, there'd always be a chance. I mean without evidence, it'd only be my word against yours, and I can tell you as a once smalltime drug dealer, the police are generally useless unless there's hard evidence. But that's not the point. I'm just trying to help you. I know it's unlikely you'll ever let me go. I'm just trying to do something positive with my last days.

Bullshit. You're trying to con me. With this cheap meditation bullshit. You take me for a fucking fool.

I know the emotions are rising now, but if you stay with it, you'll see the nature of this anger and pain.

Fuck you. You better shut the fuck up if you know what's best for you.

Digs a cigarette out of his pocket, clicks, clicks, clicks the lighter but it doesn't light.

You really pissed me off now.

On his feet. Looking around. Turns the fans back on, gust of cold pouring out. He heads out.

Could have been worse. But I fucked up. I shouldn't have gone so quickly.

He's not ready for it. He's too attached to his suffering. He can't separate himself from it.

He'll come around. He has to.

Footsteps. He returns, a cigarette smoking in his lips. Bottle of vodka.

He strides over to me, shrink back, but he grabs my blanket and tears it out of my grip. Throws it in the corner, douses it in vodka, lights his cigarette again, holds the lighter there until the flame consumes the end of the cigarette, then tosses the burning thing onto the blanket. It goes up in flames, crackles, burning away until the alcohol's done, then it's only smoke, and even that slows, leaving a blackened mess in the corner.

There. If suffering means so little to you, we'll see how fucking enlightened you are in a few days.

Please. You'll kill me. I need food.

You'd be so lucky.

He turns the light out on his way, and while his footsteps are still going up the stairs, the speakers scream into life, pulling my foot against the cuff and injecting fresh nausea into my gut.

Movement. Something in the room. Even in the darkness and the screaming speakers and the shivering cold, I feel it. Senses heightened to the slightest change.

It's him. Must be.

I stare where the door should be. Blink. Blink. Try to spot the changing darkness where his shadow moves.

Stroking my arms again. Stop it. It's pathetic. Scratch at them instead. Scratch until my fingertips are moist with blood. But I don't feel the pain. The real pain is so much deeper.

Wipe my fingers on my chest and plug my fingers in my ears, watch the darkness.

There's nothing there. You're just tripping yourself out. It's just the music. That's all you heard.

But I felt something. Someone.

You're out of your fucking mind. You wish someone was here. He'll probably leave you for a week. Probably up there drinking himself into a coma and plotting ways to hurt you even more. Maybe one day he'll drink so much he doesn't wake up. You'll be stuck in this hell as your life wastes away. And it'll take forever. One of the worst deaths you can imagine.

Should've taken the bridge when you had the chance. It would have been so quick and easy.

My torso shudders, and I kick my legs out at nothing.

It's okay, Sam.

I jerk around, reaching for the source of the voice. Her voice. But there's only wall behind me.

Jesus. It was out there, in the room, not just my mind.

What's the difference?

Talk to me. Tell me something else. Please.

Only the overlapping death growls, distorted guitars, blast beats on too many drums.

If I've lost my mind, fine. It's inevitable, isn't it? But at least be here with me. Sit with me. Talk to me like old times.

How do you know I'm not here? If you don't reach out and find nothing, how do you know?

You're here. Back to the wall, cross-legged. In a black dress. But I can't see your face.

Forget about my face.

I just want to see you smile again.

Well we both know that's not possible.

I'm sorry.

I know. You've said it a thousand times. Actually, to tell the truth, I'm getting a little tired of hearing it.

Okay, well I won't say it again.

Good.

I thought I was getting through to him.

He's complicated. We all are. It was never going to be simple like you thought.

So how do I reach him?

Why are you asking me?

I don't know, I thought... I don't know. Never mind.

You're overthinking everything.

I know, but how can I not? I have to.

Why?

If I don't think this through properly, it'll cost me my

140

life. Or worse.

And thinking is the way out of it?

I don't know. Maybe not.

You already know what you need to do. Thoughts are only echoes.

I'm scared. I don't know how it'll turn out.

We're always afraid of the unknown.

I know. But how do we avoid it?

What makes you think we need to?

I guess fear can be good. But not too much. Too much paralyses us. What if I freeze up and I can't act when the time comes?

Who is there to act or not to?

You're right. I know. I just... yeah, you're right. I'm just wasting energy. Better not to think. Just be. Just be with the endless noise and the cold and the pain and the illness. If there's no one here to feel it, it can't hurt me.

He's right. If suffering does nothing to impede enlightenment, if it even enhances it, I can bear it. I can bear anything. I've seen through it before. I see it now.

Let it sustain itself. Get out of your own way.

And then when he eventually does come back, you know what to do.

Plug my ears for just a moment's break from the assault, but it barely changes the effect. Hold my head in my hands, massage my scalp for comfort. Fingertips brushing my hair.

I have hair now. Proper hair. More than just a fuzz of an overdue shave.

Jesus, how long have I been down here?

The music stops, jerking me back to my body. Silence now but the horrible noise lingers in my stomach, in my trembling muscles, my screaming headache.

His footsteps thunder down the steps and he bursts into the room. Snaps on the light and slams the door behind him. Stands there glaring at me. Breathing heavy.

I have to close my eyes to keep from throwing up.

He moves closer. I steal a look through squinted eyes. He's searching the shelves for something. Buys me another few seconds.

Massage my closed eyelids, look for my breath. Inhaleexhaleinhaleexhale.

Got to look again. Got to look again.

He stands still, staring down at me. Holding a butcher's handsaw.

No.

He smiles, steps towards me. Nothing I can do to stop him. I shrink back but there's only wall.

Please. I can help you. You don't want to do this.

Don't tell me what I fucking want.

He steps in, leans over, and grabs hold of my arm. I try to pull his wrist away, and he backhands me with the fist holding the saw.

A star implodes in my head, everything ringing and faint. Nausea burning in my stomach.

He thrusts his knee into my gut and his weight forces me back to the floor. Can only hold his arm holding mine but my muscles are empty.

He slides his knee up to my chest, his leg across my neck pinning me. He positions my arm and surveys it like a workman examining his line before he makes the cut. Rests the blade on my forearm, just below the elbow, and starts to saw.

The sharp teeth bite, slice my skin open. Blood comes to the surface and runs down my arm. I feel the wetness before the pain arrives. Burning, screaming pain like nothing else I've felt. And still sawing sawing. Gripping my arm like a vice to keep it in place. I resist with all my strength but only slow his hand for a second.

He grits his teeth, heavy breath warming my face. Look of fixed concentration, like his life depends on the task at hand. Blood droplets hit his face and stay there, abstract warpaint.

I can't keep the cry out of my throat. A boy's wail echoes around the room. He's through skin now, cutting into muscle. Nausea like a black hole in my gut. Vomit waiting for a spare second to come up.

Blood running continuously. My whole arm on fire. Muscle contracting as if trying to get away from the path of the saw. Reddy-pink amidst the blood. Just like a piece of meat and a butcher cutting into it. No feeling. Empty eyes, focused only on the task at hand.

Fucking monster. Psychopath. Kill him. Need to kill him.

Get my fingers up into his face, in his eyes, try to push him away, but he turns his head to slip away from my fingers, and bites my hand.

I pull it back, but it snaps to his arm again as soon as he resumes sawing.

The blade scrapes against bone, and he doubles down, arm moving in longer, faster strokes.

Get it over with.

The sound of metal on bone and blood flowing flowing down my arm, pooling on the tiles, running down the grout channels. Ears ringing and head growing airy.

Don't fight it. Just let it happen. It'll be over soon.

I'll bleed out. He'll kill me.

Good. The end's in sight. Then no more pain. No more suffering. And you know you won't really die.

My head falls back against the floor. Close my eyes. Watch the breath. Inhale. Pain burning, getting deeper and deeper. Exhale. Through the bone now. Not long. Pain fresh again. He grunts to himself. Like I'm not even here. Lifeless flesh and blood.

Finally he breaks through. A wet slap as my arm hits the floor. Blood leaking out of the stump. From severed veins and arteries. Mangled muscle and exposed bone. Skin hanging off like sausage casing. My forearm lies there on the tiles like some optical illusion, streaked with blood, the knuckles still scabbed over from punching the wall.

Everything getting foggy now. He steps back, says something but it doesn't reach me. Vomit trying to work its way up my throat, but the muscles don't work properly.

Everything dizzy and faint, racing backwards through a tunnel.

Let this be it. Please let this be it. Don't let me wake up.

My limbs spread on the wet floor, some instinctive imitation of the Vitruvian Man.

Inhale. Exhale. In-

My whole body groans as I roll over. Head thumping like double bass drums.

Jesus Christ, I'm still here. Still alive.

Now the groan comes from my mouth.

Have to suffer this all again. The pains old and new. Can't bear it.

But you can.

My stump of a leg. The worst source of pain. Bend my knee and pull it round to face me. The sight of it nearly makes me vomit. Swallow it back. Wrapped in peeling skin, the mangled reddy-pink flesh, spotted with green and white, like a big rotting sausage. Severed arteries in the mix, drained of their life force.

One of the arteries squirms, emerges an inch from the stump, then retreats back inside. Not an artery. A worm. I shiver with disgust, feel it move amongst the pain.

I pinch my fingers inside the stump, hold it still with my free hand, leg aching, but the worm slips through my fingertips. Wipe them off on my thigh and try again. I grip it with my nails and draw it out. The bloody inches keep coming and coming, twice the length I was expecting, three times. Like a sick magic trick. Must have been all the way up by my hip. Or coiled inside my leg.

I fling it away. It slaps the wall and falls to the floor, squirming as if in pain.

My stomach kicks but nothing comes up. The revulsion slowly leaves my body and I find my breath again.

144

The handcuff lies on the floor beside my severed foot, dried blood everywhere. Just seeing it makes me feel faint again, but it passes. I'm not dead yet. I'm free. Of the shackle at least. The door will be locked, but I'm free of the first and hardest layer of the prison.

Didn't think I'd survive, did you, motherfucker?

I drag myself with aching arms along the blood-stained tiles to the door. Door's definitely locked, but I can maybe break through it. There must be a tool in here.

Drag myself back to the shelving units, use the frame to pull myself to my good leg. It shakes, holding my weight, barely supports me. It hasn't needed to for so many months. Jesus, is that how long it's been? Must be.

I hold onto the shelving, try to ignore the pain and trembling. Check the boxes. Spare brackets and screws, cables. Mole grip. Where's the hammer? There are screwdrivers, wire strippers, tape measure. There. On the other shelf. I hop over, grab the shelf for support, take the hammer, drop back to the ground. My open stump scrapes the tile and I yell out. Shut up. He'll hear. Bite the back of my hand to silence myself.

Breathe through the pain. It's okay. Just a minute.

Come on. We don't have time. Back to the door. What am I supposed to do? If he heard me yell out, he'll definitely hear me attacking the door. Although maybe not. There are at least a couple doors between me and him and a set of stairs. Unless he does have a microphone or camera hidden in the room. Have to take the chance. Won't get it again.

Hop a step, two, then go to my bum and drag myself the rest of the way. Onto my good knee, supporting myself on the wall. Raise the hammer and bring it down hard on the handle. Again and again, taking a chip out of it, rocking it, missing the handle and hitting the door itself. I'll smash my way through the wood if I have to.

No, you won't. You don't have the energy for it.

Hit the handle again and again. The handle breaks cleanly off, the exposed lock nested in the door. I can turn it with a tool. Pliers maybe. There must be something I can use.

Back to the floor, dragging myself to the shelving. Give my leg a break. But the exhaustion's already getting to me. Getting lightheaded. I slip in the blood and knock my head. Should have been dry. Fuck. I'm so weak. Need some water. Was there any left?

Inhale. Exhale.

There's a little in the bottle by the wall. It's not enough, but if you rest a moment, you'll feel better.

Don't have time to rest. Need to move. Need to get the fuck out of here.

Back to the shelves. Would the mole grip work? Probably not. A screwdriver? Maybe. There's nothing else that would work. Take two.

I drag myself over the floor, toss the screwdrivers ahead to free my second hand. Cross the floor. Get the screwdrivers in the square hole of the deadlock, try to turn it. The lock fights back, but I grit my teeth and tense my whole body, get it open.

The stairs stretch above me. Listen. No sounds from the house. Maybe only a faint buzzing.

Bite hold of the smaller screwdriver and drag my weight up the steps. So much heavier than the basement floor. Have to stop. Just another step. Now rest a second. Inhale. Exhale. Listen again.

Silence from the house.

The air's different here. Smells different. A passageway between two worlds, infused with a mix of both atmospheres.

Got to move again. Don't have time. Deep breath. Two more steps. Three more. Only four left. You can do it, Sam. What if this door's locked too?

Just get to the top. Come on. One more step. One more. One more.

Try the handle. It's open. Thank God. Okay, quiet. He could be anywhere.

Slowly push the door in, move into the hallway, push the door back to, close it silently. Jaw aching from the screwdriver. Take it out and move forward on my arse and free arm. Quieter this way. There's a little daylight in the house. A window down the hallway, front door. My heart jolts. But another door open on the right before I get there. I slow down, making no sound at all, inch my head around the door frame.

It's him.

Fuckfuckfuck. Freeze up, gripping the screwdriver so tight it shakes. All my energy channelled into my wrist.

He's asleep. Bottles of beer and spirits strewn across the table.

The door. Try the door.

Back up slowly, keeping him in sight until I'm at the door, try the handle. Locked obviously. He'll have the keys. On his person if not somewhere in the house. Probably on him.

Get them. You have the upper hand. Screwdriver him in the neck to immobilise him, then get the keys from his pocket. And if they're not there, you're free to search the house.

But I don't have the energy. I barely got up here. If he fights back or even touches my stump, I won't stand a chance. And then it'll be back to the basement, the chain on my other foot and all over again, the endless loops, the music, dark, light, cold, the aches and pains and never sleeping.

Kill him.

It'll be easy. Quick. But be quiet. Don't make a sound or you'll wake him. Screwdriver back in the teeth and low to the ground, sharing my weight between my arms and bum. Knees into my chest with the stump staring up at me.

Worm wriggling.

Gently. Don't knock the coffee table. Grip the screwdriver.

Do it. He's right there. Defenceless. Probably drank

himself into a coma.

Put it in his neck.

Let me see if I can get the keys first. If he goes for me, I'll kill him.

Up on my knee. Reach out and touch his pocket. There's a vague bulge there. Maybe his wallet? Don't feel keys, but maybe they're on the other side of the wallet.

Try his other pocket.

He's half-lying on it. I feel the top of his leg. There's something in there too. Keys or change. He moves, exposing the pocket, on the edge of arousal. Looks at me.

Give me the keys. Just give me the fucking keys and I won't hurt you.

But he grabs my arm, pushes me back against the table before I can stab him. I smack him in the face, cover his face with my splayed fingers, manage to slip off his grasp. I thrust the screwdriver at his throat, but he grabs me again and directs the point into the sofa. I get my foot under me and wrestle the screwdriver away. He punches me in the head, rocks me back, but he's not blocking his torso and I get the screwdriver in him. In his spleen or his kidney or liver or something. Some mystery organ. The breath goes out of him and now all he can think about is the screwdriver sticking out of him. Stares at it in horror.

Give me the fucking keys. I know you've got them.

He grabs my throat with one hand, holds the screwdriver handle ready to pull it out.

Don't let him. Grab his hand on the handle, push it in and twist. He yells out.

I'm not playing. He grabs hold of your hand. If he pulls it out, he'll die quicker. The acid and toxins will flood his blood faster than it already is. He'll be done in minutes, the life already going out of him.

But it's going out of you too. Fucking exhausted. Could pass out at any second.

Can't just leave him in case he gets the screwdriver out and uses it against me.

He glances desperately around, spots my stump, then grabs hold of it.

Pain sears through me like a hot pan hissing against it. I bite it down, jaw aching, my tooth probably cracking, go for the screwdriver and yank it out of him. His hand on me but doing nothing. Paralysed puppetmaster. As the pain burns away, I direct the screwdriver back into him, into his upper thigh.

He throws his head back, hissing.

Get those fucking keys. Go in his pocket and grasp them. He moves to stop you, but he's too slow from the pain. He's done.

They jingle as I draw them out. He doesn't care. He's writhing about on the sofa, trying to shift the pain and the knowledge of what's coming for him.

I leave the screwdriver in him, leave him to die, back to the floor, make for the front door. He stays where he is.

Get the key in the door. Turn it. Try the door. Still locked. Another lock. Change keys and unlock that one, shift back from the door and open it.

The light disappears down the stairs. Back to the basement. No, something must be wrong. I got the wrong door.

The hallway leads back to where I came up. He's still slumped back on the sofa, his hands laid across his wounds and staring blankly up at the ceiling.

Why would he have a staircase outside of his front door? Hop back down the hallway, but the door I came up leads down just the same. There must be another way out. A window. Somewhere upstairs.

Back down the hallway, forcing the breath in. Willing muscles not to give in. Sit on the stairs and drag myself up step by step. All dark outside and in. For a second the world spins and I'm going down the stairs. Dizzy and nauseous. Need to rest.

Give up.

I don't know why you do this to yourself.

You know this isn't real.

Don't tell him. He doesn't need to know.

There's no way out. Not like this.

Just watch the mind a minute.

Lay my head on the carpeted step. Fish bowl spilling water. Panting and heart thumping.

I don't want to go on.

Don't. It's okay. Just sleep. Leave this tortured vessel for a time. This body is not your only body.

But I can't. It needs me. I need to protect it.

It doesn't need you. And you don't need it.

The walls dissolve and you feel the spacious air. Your physical signature fragments like a slow shotgun spread, mixing with thoughts, sensations that don't belong to you. Other times and other lives. And it doesn't matter. This is one frame among infinite possible frames.

You're old. You're young. You're born. You die. Always switching frames. Moving, always moving, so you don't stop to question it. And the memory of her across all of it. Lurking in the back of each frame. Face blotted out by him. By me. And then you forget even that. You are the content and the context both. All of it at once and it's bliss. But that too passes. Don't hold on. It comes freely. You can't cling to it.

The bliss interspersed by waves of pain and guilt and longing. The gravitational pull of being.

Let it happen.

I can't.

Let it do its thing. Nirvana and samsara depending on each other. One and the same. You know this.

Stay with the breath, Sam.

The breath? What is the breath? Meaningless. Even your breath will fail one day, and then what will you hold onto?

If there is to be a watcher, it's the best thing to watch.

But who says there's a watcher? That's you. You're doing that.

Something so simple, the mere movement of air in and

out of my body. The cool air on my nostrils. My chest rising and falling faintly like lazy waves. The small pleasure, compared to the infinite nothingness, ecstasy a single flame glowing in the darkness. I'll live out every second of this life here with nothing but the breath to occupy me.

But you can't. There's so much more suffering to do.

So let me leave this place. I'll scatter myself across the universe and wake in a haze of amnesia, new lives to lead, round and round, everything at a hundred miles an hour and never stopping to think about it, but in dreams, deep in dreams never remembered, I'll know the truth.

So do it. Live your infinite lives, but you'll still suffer out there. And you know you'll always come back here eventually. Isn't it better to just live it now? Live it with love and compassion and bring a little light to the darkest of places?

He's not capable of it. He's not ready.

You'll see.

I'm so cold, my body's starting to shut down. Even the shaking is going. Never thought that'd be a bad thing. Need the blanket. There must be something left.

I crawl into the corner and feel around for it. Draw it to me. Smells awful. Burnt fabric, covered in ash, several big holes in it. Smell of piss and shit as well.

Better than nothing.

I wrap it around me, lie back on the ground. Stinks and feels nasty on my skin, open wounds. No trace of the comfort it first brought.

It's this or die from cold.

I thought maybe we'd try some mettā today.

Meta?

It's a type of meditation. It's pretty straightforward, don't worry. But it can be good for… easing suffering I guess. For positive feelings.

Okay.

Okay, so just start like normal. Close your eyes and find the breath. Just breathing normally. Not willing the breath but just watching it with a little curiosity. Feeling it in our abdomen or chest or nostrils.

And when we get lost in thought, we just notice, without judgement, and come back to the breath.

Okay, now you're settled, I'd like you to visualise someone. A friend. Someone for whom you have positive feelings.

His wife? Mina? Or do they only bring pain now? He shouldn't think of them.

Not necessarily someone you're really close with, but just someone who makes you feel happy. A Good friend.

I get it.

Visualise them happy. Smiling, laughing. Completely absorbed in the moment.

And then wish them happiness.

May you be happy.

But you only need to think it.

Imagine them smiling.

May you be at peace. And recognise you really want this to be true. You care about this person and you want them to be happy and not depressed or in pain.

Mm.

May you be free from suffering.

Does he feel it? He must feel something. He must have empathy at least for those he loves. Or is there no one he loves anymore? Is there no space for compassion in all the hate?

May you be free from hatred.

May you be free from ignorance.

May you be free from physical pain and illness.

You can repeat any words you like, but those are the ones I usually use. Repeat them a few times as you try to visualise the person.

Steal a glance. He has his eyes closed, but he's still all tensed up.

And now, I want you to think about a new person. Someone who's neutral to you. Someone you don't really know. A shop assistant or a local dog-walker or someone like that. Someone you don't have particularly positive or negative feelings about. But a specific person. Try to visualise them. Imagine them happy. And again repeat the phrases.

May you be happy.

May you be at peace.

May you be free from suffering.

May you be free from hatred.

May you be free from ignorance.

May you be free from physical pain and illness.

Leave him with it for a moment.

And then we move on to a person we don't like.

Me.

Someone we have negative feelings for.

You. He's obviously thinking of you. You set him up for that one.

And then you visualise them.

Throat getting scratchy. I clear it. Sneak a glance, but he's looking too. Quickly close my eyes. Breathing faster.

You try to imagine them being happy and at peace.

And you repeat the phrases.

May you be happy.

May you be at peace.

May you be free from suffering.

You think I don't know what you're doing?

I'm just trying to help you.

You fucked it. You pushed it too hard and lost him.

You want me to imagine you all happy and blissful and realise that actually, I don't really want you to suffer and it's not helping me anyway, so why don't I just let you go?

I thought we'd been through this.

So did I. So I don't know why you're trying to pull this bullshit again.

Okay, I'm sorry. It's just part of the meditation. We can

skip the negative person. The final person is yourself. So you just try to imagine yourself happy and smiling, lost in the moment. Or you can remember a specific time where you were really happy and absorbed.

Before you entered my life. That's when I was happy.

I know. I'm sorry. So humour me for a moment. Please. Remember the moment. And recognise that you want yourself to be happy.

Obviously.

And you want the younger version of yourself to be happy. There's no part of you that wishes you could go back in time and be unhappy in that moment.

And then just repeat the phrases again, about yourself. The versions of yourself you came through to get here in this moment and the versions of yourself yet to come.

May you be happy.

May you be at peace.

May you be free from suffering.

May you be free from hatred.

May you be free from ignorance.

May you be free from physical pain and illness.

Check him. Eyes closed. Looks calmer. Is that the hint of a smile?

Are we done?

Yeah.

Good.

He gets up, makes for the door, patting his pocket for his cigarettes. Pauses in the doorway for a second but doesn't say anything, turns away.

Kills the light.

Got a light?

Oh. Yeah. Here.

She relights the joint, inhales, leans her head back against the wall and slowly exhales. Eyes closed. Looks so peaceful.

Hands the joint to me. Should I hit this? What difference does it make?

Inhale. Exhale.

It just goes on and on, doesn't it?

That's the fun of it.

Fun? This is fun to you?

You're missing the big picture. You always were so myopic.

My vision is getting dreadful.

That's not what I meant.

I know.

When there is light, you'll see again.

Not in this life.

What is a life to us?

It's something.

Yes. But there are so many more to live.

It's true. And some of them must be pretty nice.

Some are delightful.

And some of them horrifying.

Worse than this.

Really? Worse than this?

A few. I didn't stay long.

That makes me feel a bit better, to think even now, after all of this, it could be worse. That's a bit twisted, isn't it?

I don't know. I don't think so.

What could be worse than this anyway?

Use your imagination.

I relight the joint, hit it again, and pass back.

Maybe not right now.

No. Not now.

Exhales. Eyes closed.

What are you thinking?

She smiles. Why do I have to be thinking something?

Good point.

I close my eyes too. Exhale. Let myself just be. Let the being be.

Have you ever done acid? Or other psychedelics?

Once when I was younger. But I didn't have a very good

time with it. Why do you ask? Obviously you have.

I was curious. And because of the water I thought... And it's how a lot of people first break into spirituality. I don't think I'd have pursued this path, or even started meditating if it weren't for psychedelics. You know Mina was into it, meditation I mean. She knew the benefits. She was the one that kind of spurred me on, I guess.

I didn't know that. I knew she was into her crystals and incense and she did a bit of yoga, but I didn't know she meditated.

Surveys me with suspicion for a second, as though considering if I'm lying, what are you hiding? then settles. Lights a cigarette.

Offers me one.

Thanks.

So you want me to do acid too? Soften me up to be more like you?

I'm not suggesting anything. Under the wrong circumstances, it could even make things worse. I just thought it was worth mentioning.

I think I'll stick to the meditation for now.

We smoke in silence. It rushes to my head, makes my throat scratchy. I drink a little water. Not much left. Cover myself.

The high is more like cocaine than tobacco in my exhausted, hypersensitive state. The whole room coming into focus and him just sitting there smoking, thinking. Or maybe thinking nothing. Does he have the capacity to be absorbed in the moment and not identified with any one thought or sight or sensation? Not until he can meditate properly. Although everyone must have moments of it, even without realising what they're experiencing.

Or he's plotting some nasty scheme to catch me off guard and torture me all the more.

Thinking about her.

He believes we were friends now. I actually knew her, not just some faceless character who sold her dirty drugs through a car window. Knowing that she meditated too, that's got to motivate him more. But I can't move too fast or he thinks I'm trying to manipulate him. Aren't you? He has to feel that it's his decision, that he's in control.

We'll see about that.

He needs it. I'm supposed to help him. I was always supposed to. Maybe that's why I'm here. Maybe some unconscious part nudged him when he heard I was a Buddhist. Maybe he thought I could save him. Some hazy hope that we'd find ourselves in a situation like this right here.

A little idealistic don't you think? A little mystical? That's not how kamma works. And you studied psychology, when you weren't getting high and selling drugs I mean, but you know motivation and behaviour aren't that simple.

It's a nice idea. Maybe it helps me.

Maybe. But you shouldn't lie to yourself.

It's not lying. Just playing with possibilities. Exaggerating the odds a little.

Look, choose whatever reality you want. It really doesn't matter in the end.

No. It doesn't.

I don't feel good. Something feels wrong. Still gritty from the pills and the mushrooms starting to hit too early. Nausea still nesting in my stomach. Head swimming a little. I look around, a camera panning at low frame rate. Too much information for my brain to compute. Disconnecting from the different Sams in the lost frames. Ears ringing.

There is no consistent me. Each new fraction of experience, however arbitrarily divided, is a new me. At any moment, a new me could slip through and take the reins and I'd be gone and what if I never come back?

Think I might be sick. I'm in a state. It's too loud here. The speaker stacks blasting at me from multiple angles. The screaming and distortion are too much. Feel the vibration in my tissue.

Should get back. Get somewhere safe where I can just lie down and ride this shit without passing out and being robbed or dragged into a bush and raped.

I'd fucking kill him.

But I can barely stand up. Gravity stronger than it should be. Balance tries to adjust. Head pulses. Stomach kicks. A little sick works its way up, but I swallow it back down. Shouldn't have drank so much water. I'll have to pee soon, but I can barely see, barely coordinate my movement.

Come on. Just move before you lose the ability.

Every step drains the tank. So tired and out of it. I shouldn't have done the mushrooms. Or smoked on the comeup.

As I get further from the stage, the music from the second stage gets louder, competes with the first. Both of them loud as each other, both screaming at me, drums blasting over each other. Rhythms twisting in and out of each other. The ground rumbling with all the vibration. So disorientating.

I pass a crowd, revealing a few people behind them kneeling around a body. Next to the dumpster, a girl seizing on the ground, her legs kicking out like she's trying to tread water in the air, eyes staring out at me but tracking something in another world entirely.

Must be fucked on drugs. There's always one. Or maybe she just gets seizures. Epileptic. All the flashing lights and loud music. Probably drugs though. Some nasty batch. Dealers get greedy at festivals. Lack of accountability.

She'll be okay. Just keep moving. You need to get back to the tent before you end up like her. Just get back. Where it's quiet and safe. Forget the toilets. You can piss in a bottle if you have to.

Okay, up the hill. Legs aching. Just breathe. Inhale. Exhale. Music a bit quieter up here.

I'll probably have to be sick too. Can lie with my head out the tent and be sick on the ground.

Just pray you don't pass out first. I'll need to lie on my

side. Can't choke on my vomit. That's how they get you. That's how they get you.

Head like a bowling ball. Legs aching. Protesting. Can't take much more. You really fucked us here.

Okay, then rest. Sit. Just for a few seconds. Might need to be sick here. They'll watch, laugh, but nothing I can do about that. My stomach burns, blood pumping in my head, working overtime to keep the lights on. Keep me here. So exhausted, just want to rest, sleep.

An endless stream of legs and boots past my eye line. So many people. See, they're just like you. You're nothing special. Just carbon copies of each other. Jeans and band-shirt-wearing drug-taking hedonistic nihilists. You could die and there'd be thousands to take your place. Smarter, richer, better-looking, funnier, more successful copies.

Pair of legs walking slower than the rest, barely impeded by the stream. He slows, almost to a stop, staring sideways at me. Big bulbous bear head, grey fur with patches of muddy brown. One beady eye missing. Just the hole with the real guy's eye staring out. He studies me, sussing out my potential weakness. Alone and barely keeping it together. It's dark and I'm fucked on drugs. There's at least a couple hundred and a few baggies in my bag. He could take it all, and I'm so exhausted, I probably couldn't stop him. He's a big guy. I made myself too vulnerable.

He moves on, drifting round the corner. Could be lingering, but I keep an eye out.

What the fuck was his problem? Wearing a mask isn't so bad. It's a festival. People wear masks at festivals. But fun, quirky shit. Maybe he just wants to disguise himself. The anonymity that grants all permissions. He's up to no good.

Or maybe I'm just paranoid. Could be the mushrooms and weed twisting my mind. I only saw him for a second. But it felt real. There was something wrong about him. And the girl seizing. Maybe she just primed me. Jesus, my head. Try to look around, and my vision pans in choppy low frame rate.

Okay, got to move, Sam. Not much longer now.

Just one leg after another. Focus on the task at hand.

Shutting down other processes to preserve mental functioning. Emotions. Short-term memory. Social awareness. Just the one task held in mind: get to the tent. You know the route. Navigating crowds coming the other way. Avoiding obstacles. Legs burning. The movement keeping the nausea down. Looking only at where I'm going, wide vacant stare. I must look hypnotised. It's just the tiredness. And the drugs. I can't be the only one.

Turn the corner into our area. Find our row, look for my tent. Get it unzipped and crawl inside.

People shouting down the row. Metal blasting from a nearby speaker. Laughing. People talking a couple of tents down. Shove my rucksack down into the bottom of the tent and stretch out on top of my sleeping bag. Stomach churning from the movement. Taste the sick at the other end of the pipe. It's coming. Surges up. Burning my throat. Streams out. Manage to get the grass. No one's around to see. But they'll see the pool when they come back.

A second round. My stomach and throat burning. Scratchy. Cough. Need some water, but I drank it all. Too far to walk for it. Head pounding.

Slither back into my tent. Voices moving closer. A guy and girl. Mina? No, it couldn't be. Just some stranger.

God, my head. So tired. Close my eyes to rest. Preserve energy. But it's too dizzying. Just have to lie here. Shadows passing over the tent, voices suddenly several feet away through the tent, then moving on. Endless bodies, any one of whom could have nefarious intentions. Statistically speaking, there'll be so many here. These places attract criminal opportunists.

You're one yourself.

But I wouldn't hurt anyone. Steal or rape. I'm just a solo entrepreneur. It's just business.

And what if someone you sell to gets really fucked up and gets hospitalised or dies?

My product's fine. It wouldn't be my fault. People can die on good product. Take too much. Lack of sleep and not drinking water. People have to be responsible for themselves. I can't make all their decisions for them. If they don't drink water and they take drugs when they really shouldn't, that's on them.

Like you? Look at the state you're in. Even with your tolerance. And you're supposed to be smart. Not everyone is so wise.

I know. Shut up. They have to make their own decisions. People can get themselves in deadly states from booze too. And they can buy booze right from the bars. Crates of beer and litres of spirits decanted into plastic bottles and brought with them. If the big drinks companies can profit, why can't I? It's only fair. I know the risks, and I'm careful.

Can't be too careful.

Girl yells out. Laughter.

Music changes. More screaming.

Went too hard. Fucked it for myself. Can't even sleep with all this noise. Could plug my ears and close my eyes, but then I'm vulnerable to getting robbed. No friends around now.

Just paranoid. Losing your head.

Close your eyes. Rest. Watch the breath. Laboured still but slowly easing. The mushroom disorientation settling a little. Shapes and patterns coming to the fore. A plane of eyes, looking right at me. Sussing me.

I stare at myself in the mirror.

Eyes gaping. Seeing everything and nothing.

Who are you? Hm? Who exactly do you think you are?

I'm me.

Sam. Samuel.

That's who you think you are?

Yeah, motherfucker.

Haha. Hahahaha. Stupid shit. Arrogant too.

I open the door, but it pulls out of my grasp and slams

shuts again. Someone pulled it from the other side.

Hey.

I open it again. No one there.

Obviously. You're hallucinating. Tripping balls.

Haha yeah. I am. Can't deny this is some crazy shit.

Door opens and he comes in. Light on. Silence.

Wearing a rainjacket with a black rucksack over his shoulder. A little dishevelled. He's been outside. Must have just got back.

He slumps in the chair. Eyes a little unfocused, probably from drinking. Goes in his bag and breaks a can of Budweiser off the fourpack and cracks it open. Drinks. Sees me. Breaks off another can and offers it to me.

Really?

I shuffle over and take it.

Thank you.

He shrugs, goes in his pocket for a cigarette.

I open the beer and drink. Cold and refreshing. God, I never thought I'd get to taste beer again. Maybe I shouldn't drink, but there's water in it. Feels good. And it's a way of getting him onside. Turning him down would only distance me from him. It's not that I'm better than you, but I've seen how intoxication of the mind obscures the truth. That's not who I am anymore.

But you're drinking. You'd smoke if he offered it.

But it's not who I really am. I'm beyond that. To the point where it doesn't really matter to me what happens out there in reality. What happens in here, in awareness is free from that grasping.

If you say so.

Dopamine hitting my brain. Relaxing me.

I'm guessing it's late in the evening, but I'm quite awake. Slept a little before.

How are you doing?

Looks at me.

Fine.

Drinks his beer. Smokes his cig.

The weather's getting shitty. You don't feel the cold?

I feel it.

He nods. Pulls out his phone and stares at it, scrolling intermittently.

You want to come up to the house for a drink? There's a fight on I'm gonna watch.

Me? Come up?

Go. You have to go.

What if it's a trap?

He shrugs.

Okay. Yeah. Thanks.

Alright. Give me a minute.

He gets up, tosses his cigarette butt away, and heads out. Leaves the door open a crack. My heart jumps.

This could be my chance.

Need to be careful. He'll be expecting it. He'll be ready for an escape attempt. And then I'll just make things worse for myself. He won't trust me again. Probably just continue the torture indefinitely.

He's drunk. And lonely. He's not quite on the ball. And when he slips up, you seize the opportunity. This is not the time to fuck around being overly cautious. You get an opening, you fucking take it.

Do what you have to do.

Footsteps on the stairs. He returns with a new cream blanket, no just a duvet cover. He hands it to me, and I wrap it around my tired limbs, taking it slow around the most damaged parts of this old body. Not even old. Just wasted. He takes out a keychain, goes to one knee.

Stares me dead in the eyes, holds my gaze. I'm in power here. Do anything to try and challenge me, I'll kill you.

He unlocks the cuff and it springs open. I draw my foot back, into space it shouldn't have. Gently rub the raw, abused skin where the cuff did its worst.

He straightens up, walks to the door, then waits for me.

Get to my feet, walk slowly to him on shaking legs. He

leads us up the stairs, always staying a couple of paces ahead. I couldn't keep up with him if I tried. My legs barely holding my weight. Using my hands on the walls.

He opens the door and light spills down. He disappears around the corner. Last couple of steps. A corridor. He pauses in a doorway at the end.

Close the door behind you.

I close it, shutting a second Sam down there. Can't think about that right now. This could be my chance.

I follow him into the living room. Dimly lit. A black leather sofa, armchair, small table and chairs in the corner, big widescreen TV mounted on the wall. Kitchenette in the back.

Does he live here? Looks more like a badly taken care of second home, B&B maybe? Is he rich enough to afford that?

Sit.

He gestures at the chair in the corner. Not good enough for the sofa. Doesn't want me getting it dirty. I sit and rearrange the sheet about me. Sip my beer.

He turns on the TV, tunes to the fight. Just pre-amble at the moment. Finishing reels from the fighters.

He stands in front of the TV, then turns quickly as if remembering something. His drink. He drains the beer and goes in the kitchenette for a bottle and a whisky glass. Two.

He pours the whisky, carries mine over. I guess he's taking me along for the ride. Deeper into his world.

But my body can't take it. I'm so weak and tired, the alcohol hits me more than it should. Goes straight to my brain. He's used to it, probably soak it up with a carby meal while I starve like a neglected dog.

He settles on the sofa, lights a cigarette. Sits forward, rocking his foot up and down.

Fighters getting ready. White trunks a toned Brazilian Jiu-Jitsu black belt with long arms. Black trunks a tall brawler, huge arms, tatted all over. He mimes a jab-cross-uppercut for the camera.

The referee starts them, and they're off. Throwing feints and testing each other's reach, testing reactions.

White catches black with a calf-kick. Black slides back, switches stance, and lands a quick jab-cross.

He knocks back his whisky, and I copy him without thinking. The whisky burns, my stomach protests, but then a pleasant warmth, a floatiness.

Need to stay sharp. Need to be ready.

There's a window, but he's closer to it. If he goes back into the kitchen, I could dart for it, but I wouldn't be quick enough to fiddle with the handle, get it open, and climb out. I'd need more time. Even then, it's bound to be locked. He's not that stupid. Although he probably didn't plan for me being up here. Drunk and lonely. And if I get outside, then what? I couldn't run far. I have no idea where we are. Where to go.

You have to try.

Black catches white with an overhand, opens a cut above his eye. White lands a shot of his own, another calf-kick. Waits. Black goes in for another combo, and white drops down, folds black back onto the mat. They scramble and end up clinching against the fence.

Black fights to get his back off the wall and eventually breaks, earning a heavy elbow for his efforts. He goes in for a combo, but white evades, counters with a one-two.

They trade a few blows before the first round ends. Go off to their corners.

He sips his whisky, lights another cigarette. Gets up and paces, leaving the path to the window clear.

Still not enough time to reach it. Need to find out if it's locked first.

He stands a few feet from the screen, raises his fists and bobs and weaves a little. Shadowboxing some rudimentary strikes.

The second round starts and it's blows raining. Another counter-takedown, but this time black can't get up. White gets to half-guard, then mount. Throws a bomb at black's face. Black covers up, tries to turn and shrimp his hips away, but white moves with him. Pins his leg and takes his back. Gets a rear-naked choke on black, but black fights it. Manages to slip out. They get back to their feet. White gets in a leg-kick, goes for another early takedown, but black sees it coming and evades it. Lands a heavy blow. Another. Rocks white.

Ten-second mark. White sees red and goes in hard, throwing punches, landing a few, white dances away, lands a couple of his own.

Back to their corners.

He drains his whisky, pours another. Takes out a baggie and sits in the other chair beside me. Pours half the white powder onto the table, cuts it into two lines with a credit card, and snorts one with a note.

You used to deal right?

You're just as bad as me. Worse.

He knows I did. I nod.

He offers the note to me.

I shouldn't.

You have to. It's not about your morals anymore. It's only about survival. You have to keep him onside. Plus, the coke will sharpen you. It is coke, isn't it?

I hoover the line up my right nostril. It stings, burns, like glass in my nasal passage. Then the sharp surge of energy. Definitely coke. The taste of it.

He returns to the TV, third round underway.

Shadowboxing, embodying the fighter in black, or maybe imitating moves from both of them, some of his own. Demonstrating his dominance.

Don't try anything.

He'd fuck me up. What chance do I have?

His eyes are pinned to the screen. The fight's close.

Now's the chance. Check the window.

Okay. Quickly before he turns around. Lean out on my left leg. Lean as far as I can see. The curtain's half-covering it. Try it. The handle's locked. Fuck.

I'll have to smash the glass and crawl through.

You'd have to overpower him for that. Only way to get enough time. And if you're going to overpower him, you may as well just kill him.

Only if I have to. And I'm so much weaker than him. I need to catch him off guard, and I need a weapon. There's nothing here. Maybe knives in the kitchen. I couldn't just run for it. He'd still catch me.

Could I get to the kitchen, find a weapon, and get back before he noticed? It's one thing testing the window and another getting to the kitchen.

Get low to the ground.

Even then, it's so risky. And if he catches me before I can kill or at least immobilise him, he'll kill me. Worse still, throw me back in the basement with no privileges for the rest of my sorry life. All this hard work would be wasted.

But I need to get out of here. I don't know when I'll get another chance.

White and black down on the mat again. White fighting for the choke. Black escapes it, uses the opening to try to get back to his feet, but white only trades the choke for an armbar, pinning black and forcing him to tap.

The ref breaks the submission and the crowd goes crazy as white jumps to his feet, screaming into the camera.

He yells out too. Grabs his whisky and washes it down with the replay. Rolls his sleeves up.

That was fucking good. You see that?

Yeah, I saw it. Nice armbar.

That's why you don't fuck with those Brazilian guys man. Once they get you on the ground, it's game over.

He leans over the table and cuts another two lines. On his forearm, there are self-harm tramlines where he pushed his sleeve up. Red and white.

He sees me see. Grunts, draws his sleeve back down. Drinks his whisky. Takes up the rolled note and inhales a line.

Are we still trading? Could I do a second if he offers?

Can already feel the blood pumping in my head. Working overtime when I really don't have energy to spare.

But it does sharpen my thoughts.

He sets the note down in front of me.

Is that an offer?

He shrugs, sits down on the edge of the sofa, then gets up and starts pacing again. Post-fight commentary on screen.

Is he testing me? He wants to see how I fare in his world? Dragging me down to his level to see if I can rescue myself? Maybe he just wants me to suffer. Dragging me into his self-destruction.

I do the line up my other nostril. Burns even more than the first one. I touch my nose, expecting blood, but only a little snot comes back. The taste in my throat. I wash it back with whisky. Really need to drink water. But don't ask him. Not now.

He's all charged up. Looks like he wants a fight. It'd only work if I caught him unaware and put a knife in him or something.

I don't like your odds. Sounds like a suicide mission. And if that's the goal, fine, suits me just fine.

It's not.

You want to watch a movie?

Yes. Need to stay up here as long as possible. Maybe if he tires himself out, he'll even fall asleep and I'll be able to get a knife and sneak up on him.

Okay. Sure.

A horror film. Something violent.

Whatever.

He stares at me for a second, irritated about something. He grabs the remote, and the Netflix logo fills the screen for a moment before landing on the profiles page. Nat. Ian. Mina.

He never deleted their profiles. Nat must be the mum so -

Is that your name? Ian?

Don't ask me that.

He stares daggers at me, like he wants to hit me. Looks back to the TV, selects Ian, then scrolls down the movie categories.

Sorry.

But it is. Who else would it be?

He puts the controller down on the sofa beside him.

Go back to the basement.

Hey, I'm sorry man. Can't we just forget about it? Let's watch this movie.

He grabs his tumbler and hurls it at me. It explodes off the wall inches above my head, raining shards down on the table and floor.

Go. Now. I try to do one nice thing for you, and this is how you repay me. I shouldn't have let you up to start with.

I get my feet under me and move towards the door. He's on his feet too, but I've got a couple of steps on him.

Has to be now. It's either escape or back down to the basement. To prison.

Upstairs might have a weapon. Or an open window.

Go. Now.

Make for the stairs, use all four limbs to support myself and distribute the sound, hopefully buy myself another second.

Hey.

Still a couple steps to go when he spots me. His footsteps behind me on the steps, but I'm round the corner. Into the room. Close the door behind me and lean on it. Get the lock slid across, but when he kicks the door it shakes in its frame. Feeble little lock. It's not going to hold. The bathroom has a small frosted window. It opens, but it's a two-floor drop and probably too small for me to climb through. Get the cabinet open. No razors or scissors inside. No weapons.

The door breaks in with his foot behind it.

I could go for the window, but I just stand still and he grabs me and shoves me into the corridor. Slaps me across

169

the back of the head. Shoves me faster down the stairs.

I told you not to fucking try anything. You stupid motherfucker. After all I've done for you, this is how you repay me. You whisper all this bullshit about enlightenment and compassion and then you pull shit like this. We'll see how you like my new playlist when you're trying to sleep down there.

Down the corridor. Open the door to the stairway down.

I should have never listened to you.

I can't go back down there. Flashes of insects and shitting and the severed arm and eyes everywhere. Endless overlapping screams in the room and more in my head.

Can't go back.

Something clicks. My feet jerk back, I try to turn. Run back at him. Know I can't beat him but have to try.

He grabs my shoulder, my head with his other hand, throws me against the wall. Grabs me again and shoves me through the doorway. Only just manage to grab the bannister.

Okay. I'm going. I'm going. One step at a time. Fighting against my own instincts.

So many stone steps leading down. Walking to my own secret gallows. Not even an audience to revel in my agony.

We're always watching.

He forgets.

Go.

He shoves me again, too hard. My centre of gravity slips over the threshold, and I try to pull my weight back but I can't. I can only grab at him. His wrist. I hold him, enough to pull him forwards but I lose my hold and still falling, he's getting smaller but still falling forwards. My back explodes on the stairs. I try to roll with it but go over my shoulder. Hurts just as much. Something broke. He lands above me with a hard slap. My knee hits a stair, I keep rolling and hit the wall and then the door. Lie there for a second before his body hits me. My face stings from a rogue elbow. Back screaming from the initial impact, shoulder, arm, everything groaning and heaving. Several breaks probably. And my head getting hazy. Not enough oxygen. Need to breathe. Feeling sick.

He's completely silent. Unmoving. A wetness spreading onto my leg, but can't tell if it's me or him. Can't move my head or even my eyes without the dizziness. Horrible drunken swimming. Can't stand the pain. A nauseous wave emanates from my stomach, through my head, through my being. Don't want to hold on. Can't hold on.

My head falls back and hits the door and the lights dim and then go out.

Left foot. Right foot. Contact on the ground. Knowing the steps exactly.

Warm glow of light, of life, from the monastery windows. One bhikkhu or another still awake and active. Cleaning or reading or meditating.

I need to get out of here. Slip away in the night. Leave a note.

And where would you go? Can't go home. Could leave the country. Go to India or something. My savings would go a long way there. And I wouldn't have to live like a prisoner. Could probably score some weed in the streets too.

And how's that going to look?

Not much worse than being here. Plenty of people my age travel.

Just running away from your problems. Like you always do.

Thinking. Back to the walking, Sam. See how ephemeral these thoughts are, wisps of smoke already dissipating. But how easily you become captured by them.

That's why you need to do this.

I'm suffocating here.

Who is there to suffocate?

Yes, I know.

No, you don't. If you really knew, you wouldn't keep

going round and round in circles. Stop fucking about, and just recognise it once and for all.

How enlightened is that? How compassionate?

Sometimes you need to be cruel to be kind.

Did the Buddha say that?

Forget the Buddha.

Oh, I see.

What?

You're just Mara. You wear this guise of enlightenment, but it's just trickery. You don't want me to see the truth. You're just manipulating my own desires to keep me in samsara.

Do you hear yourself? You're paranoid. You'll never achieve Buddhahood if you're always turning away from nibbāna, always afraid of the possibility that everything is actually okay and you're the one creating problems for yourself at every turn. Why do you have to make it so complicated?

So what, I'm supposed to believe I'm already enlightened?

Who is there to be enlightened?

Oh yes, very fucking clever. But you know what I mean. In the conventional sense of me, Sam, this experience right here? My thoughts and my senses? Am I supposed to believe I've reached the end of the path and there's no more work to do? That there's no difference between me and Gautama?

Belief isn't the point. You're still complicating it. I don't know why you're even still trying to intellectualise it. Running these lofty philosophical ideas through your big brain, but it's no different than thinking about material things, sex or football or soap operas. Still in the hamster wheel.

Left foot. Right foot. Deep breath.

Left foot.

Right foot.

I need a cigarette.

It's dark. No one will see. Get them from your room. They're in the bottom of your bag with the lighter. Come back out here and smoke. You can meditate while you do it. Just to help calm the mind. I'll stop when I finish the pack. Won't have the opportunity to go to town for a while.

Okay, fine.

Still watch the steps.

Left foot. Right foot. Left.

Staying with the path, following the light, then down to the cabin.

Our light's on too.

Shit. He's sitting at the table. Smoking. Are those my cigarettes?

Sam.

Doesn't look up. Just staring down into his cold coffee. Cigarette smouldering in his fingers.

Sit for a minute.

He offers a cigarette. I take it and light it.

Shouldn't we go outside? They won't be happy if they find out we've been smoking in here.

Then I'll remind them their dissatisfaction is an illusion produced in their minds. And I've already started. You may as well smoke.

Yeah. Thanks.

We smoke in silence for a moment.

I'm thinking of leaving.

Oh? I thought things were going well.

Not really. I can't get out of my own head. I don't think I'm made for this life.

Do we really get to choose our lives?

He stubs his cigarette out in the ramakin, lays one hand on top of the other.

I'd like to think so. We have some control of our futures, aside from our genetics and external forces. Some locus of control.

If you want to go, then you'll go. But I'd counsel a little more patience. You can't get out of your head, but where can you go to avoid it? Wherever you go, you'll be in your mind. Until you stop trying to resist it and just be.

Mm. Easier said than done.

Of course.

Sometimes I do wonder if we're just doomed to our fates and as much as we try to struggle against it, we always end up in the same place we were always destined to be.

Struggle never helps.

Unless you're fighting for your life.

Well then you do whatever you have to.

Anything?

What are you asking?

I don't know. Forget it.

You know what you have to do. And you know what's too much. Only time will tell.

It's true. Thanks. I think I have to go now.

Alright, well, I'll be here. Until I'm not.

No, you tell him - that's bullshit. He's a fucking liar, and you know it. He owes me fifty quid and I want that shit back or he's gonna have me to deal with.

He puts the phone away and angrily scans the street, notices me.

Y'alright, pal?

Alright.

You got a smoke?

Yeah, one sec.

Go in my jacket pocket for my cigarettes, hand him one.

Cheers. And a light?

He lights the cigarette.

You're not married, are you?

Well, not yet. Engaged.

Don't get married. Women will just fuck up your life, whatever you try to do.

Mm can't live with them, can't live without them.

I could live without them. Fucking easily. But I can't leave her just yet until I get my new flat.

I see.

Draws deep on his cigarette.

Can't trust anyone these days. Everyone's just in it for themselves and doesn't give a shit about anyone else. You think someone's on your side, and then they stab you in the back or abandon you at the first sign of quick cash.

Mm. People can be shitty.

Yeah, see you understand. You and me actually know what the world's like.

Yeah man.

Hey, you got any change man? I don't think I have enough for this bus. Not the return anyway.

Yeah, I think so. Hang on.

Only have pennies. Or a tenner. I have to give him the tenner, don't I? He probably needs it more than me. Consider it karma.

Here.

Aw, thanks man. You've really made my day. God bless you, brother.

Don't worry about it.

I don't know if you believe in God. I just say that cause it's nice, isn't it? Do you believe?

I believe in some version of God, but not really the same as the fundamentalist Christians believe.

Nah, exactly mate. Those fundamentalists are just as bad as terrorists if you ask me. I reckon there's something out there that we're just not smart enough to see. But sometimes I have the feeling that it's not all an accident, that something's doing it all, you know?

Yeah. I know what you mean.

A bus rounds the corner. But not mine. Not his either. It drives past without stopping.

That was nice of you though, man. To tell the truth, it's been a pretty shitty day. My doctor's changed my meds for no reason, and my mind's been all over the place, and I got the Mrs causing trouble, and other money problems. So that really helps me out.

Glad to hear it.

God, where's this fucking bus? Never on time man.

Shouldn't be long now.

Here, you reckon I could get another cigarette for the walk home? It's gonna be a stressful evening as per usual, and I'm all out of smokes.

He's just trying his luck. He probably had money to start with. He's going to keep asking until you say no.

But it's only a cigarette. What if he is in need? Not much skin off my back.

You don't want to enable these motherfuckers. You help them once and they never let you go. Bleed you dry.

Alright.

I hand it over, and he smiles.

Thanks man, really appreciate that.

Holds his fist out and I bump it.

Bus coming now. Thank God.

Here, was nice talking to you though mate.

Fistbumps me again.

Yeah, you too.

May you be happy.

He sits downstairs, so I go up top. Phone vibrates as I get to my seat.

When are you getting home? x

Don't get married.

He doesn't know. She's different. They just don't know real love.

And you just happened to win the pairing lottery? More likely you're just deluding yourself.

Maybe. But is that so bad?

I reply, tell her I'm en route to get the car, and then coming straight home.

It's not too late. If you want your life back. Jettison the happy husband-father with his sleepless nights and screaming kids and constant stress. You'll have more time to play guitar, get high, go to gigs, maybe make it in the industry yourself. Or go and live in the Himalayas and find

God. Live a peaceful life without affairs and divorces and debt and resentment and redundancy.

It's worth a shot. Even if it blows up in my face. At least I can say I've lived.

Your funeral.

She replies: Ok. Bring roses ;) x

She'd be so lucky. Maybe if I pass a garage, but I probably won't. She was joking anyway.

How about a newly fixed car instead? ;)

Need to get off soon. Check Google Maps. Get off at the end of the road.

My phone vibrates.

You know how to romance a girl ;)

I press the stop button and wade downstairs. Get off the bus. Cross over. It's down here, isn't it? Must be round the corner.

Looks like the back of a garage. But there's no wall here. Didn't there used to be a wall?

No one's about. A light on but no machinery.

Hello?

I'm here for my car.

Movement behind me. Silhouette of a figure. Man in a balaclava.

Hey, relax man. I'm just here for my car. We don't have a problem with each other.

He comes at me. With a blade. Run. Go. Through the garage, through the front room. Another figure in a bally blocking the door.

I run back. Into the first guy. He slashes my forearm open, and I go down, bleeding on top of him. Try to push the blade away and get to my feet.

Go. Gogogo.

He grabs my ankle and stabs the knife into it. Feel the knife pinching into vein and smooth muscle. Drag my leg through the garage, but the door's shut. I push the bar, shove my shoulder into it, but it won't open and now the ballies are on me. The knife torn out of my leg and stabbed back into my hip, under my arm, in my neck. The pain screaming and screaming. You don't want to witness this. Go. Get out of here. It's too much for you. You can't handle this. Go. Now. And so sleepy, the pain unbearable, but disappearing like water down a plughole, draining and draining and gone.

Oh, it's good to see you, Sam. Come here. Give your mum a hug.

It's good to see you too.

Sorry. You don't want me blubbering all over you. But I get lonely sometimes you know, and it's so good to see you all mature now and making your way in the world.

Well I don't know about that.

Don't belittle yourself. I'm proud of you.

Well, that's alright then.

Aren't you proud of yourself? You should be.

I have my regrets.

We all do.

But I guess I've tried to live a life of peace and love.

As I raised you to.

Mm. Just took a while for it to click.

Sometimes you have to find your own path. Make your own mistakes along the way.

Some mistakes are too grave.

Maybe. But I'd say more important is what you do afterwards. When you recognise your mistake if you learn and grow from it or not. Whether you forgive yourself. And you have.

Just about.

Then hush about it. It's done.

You don't know what it is. If you knew, you'd never look at me the same way. You could never love me. You'd be wrong to love me.

I'll love you no matter what you do. Because love is not based on conditions. If it is, it isn't love. And part of me already knows what you've done. Like I said, let it go. Or you'll die still holding it.

I have. But he hasn't.

Ah. I thought you were free of him?

Sort of. It's not that simple.

Nothing is.

No. Have you heard from Dad?

What do you think?

I didn't think so. But I thought I'd ask.

Mm. We're better without him. Your dad, he didn't give you the best start in life. And I'm sorry for my part in that. I tried to raise you right, and although you copied some of his instincts, your better nature carried you through in the end. But you can't blame yourself for how he influenced you. You have responsibility for yourself, you know, but it's just karma. Cause and effect. Negativity breeds negativity, just like love and positivity do. And children just imitate what they think they should be doing. And when their behaviour's reinforced, it builds momentum. You know how it goes. But you've seen it too, how a tiny light can grow and grow and spread through everything. He's no match for you.

You need to kill him. Let him die. Or he will always have a place in your mind.

What do you think?

It doesn't matter what I think. It's already done. All you have to do now is live with it.

You know I can't let you go.

Yes. We've been through this.

Yeah. But I've been thinking, and I could maybe meet you halfway.

Oh?

Well you've been good for a while now. You've helped me a bit with my mind. It's only fair.

Okay. What are you thinking?

I can convert the back bedroom for you. I'd have to bar the window and lock you in, but at least you'd have daylight.

And a bed. Maybe a book or two to read. Maybe a kettle so you can make tea and Pot Noodles or something. More of a traditional prison I guess.

Okay. Thank you. Yeah, of course, that sounds good to me. Suits both our needs.

Mm. I need to figure out the logistics of it. It goes without saying, but I'm gonna say it anyway. You try any bullshit, you step one toe out of line, and you'll be right back down here with even less privileges. This is how it needs to be for both of us, so don't fuck this up for yourself.

No. I got it. Thank you.

Yeah. Don't mention it.

Aim my bum into the corner and shit, hear it landing in the bucket. Legs aching from the tension.

In my room, I could walk around a bit. Do pushups and situps, slowly at first, then properly as I build up my strength. As long as he doesn't find out. Would that make him angry? Trying to strengthen myself? It might if he hears it. I'd have to be quiet.

I wipe my arse on the toilet paper, drop it into the bag, and crawl back to the blanket.

Might even get to shit properly. But I won't have a toilet. He won't let me out and I doubt it'll have an en suite. Unless he plumbs me in my own little prison toilet in the room, I'll still be shitting in buckets and pissing in water bottles. Like he'd go to the effort for me.

Can you blame him?

It's hard to believe he's doing even this. Unless it's another game. Giving me false hope just to see me crash all the harder. A clever manipulation.

Don't trust him. He wants you on his side, thinking he's your own personal God who pulls the strings so benevolently. But it's because of him you're in here at all. Him alone. Without him, you'd be free to live out your life as an honest monk, maybe even a husband and father one day. He's taking all of that from you.

He took it from himself. It's all kamma at play. If it wasn't for Sam, he wouldn't be here either. Mina and her mother would be out there living the lives they were supposed to live. What about all that? A trade has to be made. That's how it's always worked. A life for a life. And still it's tipped in your favour.

In my favour?

You get to live. They didn't get that.

And this is a life, is it? All of these months, maybe even years, that I'd wish away every second of? I'd rather death.

But life doesn't care what you want. And the wanting is meaningless. Tying yourself in knots.

I know. But easy for you to say.

Your fate is in your hands. You got this far, you can go all the way. Play your part. Always with compassion in mind. Always aware. Gain his trust. Until he slips. Until you get your opening. And then you take it.

And then what?

And then you live your life.

He'd find me again.

You could go to the police.

No, I wouldn't. That's decided.

How do you know? Until you're out, behind a safely locked door, with a phone in your hand?

The score's settled. I don't care about revenge or justice anymore. I just want to be free of my prison.

But the room will be nice. Not such a bad life. The kind of life I would have had if the law had its way.

They wouldn't have convicted me.

And it's not the same. Normal prison comes with a sentence. And end date. He's never going to let me go. He wants you to be all grateful and indebted to him for your new and improved prison.

Then play the part. Become what he needs you to be. Until the time is right.

Door opens. Light on. He stands in the doorway, regarding

me. No water or food. But maybe it's time.

He crosses the room, goes to one knee, and unlocks the cuff. I pull my ankle back, nurse it. Feeling the air anew on my skin.

He stands watching for a moment.

Come on.

Holy shit, it's time.

I get up, using the wall, test my weight. Then gather my things. The blanket, empty plastic water bottle. That's it. All the possessions I own.

Fewer the better.

Easy for you to say.

He leads the way to the door and heads up the stairs. I can walk, just about, holding the wall for support.

One last look at the basement. Half-pixelated vignette with my bad sight. So much suffering and unpleasantness on that small patch of tiled floor, but there's still anxiety about leaving. The urge to crawl back into my blanket, shut my foot in the handcuff again, and tell him to let me stay. It might be shit, but it's all I know.

I kill the light, close the door behind me, and follow him up the stairs. Low ceiling almost scraping my head. Holding onto the wall. Up and up, and then another door and a hallway. He stops before the front door, waits for me to hobble a couple of steps, then gestures up the stairs.

I grab the bannister and pull myself up the stairs, panting, everything aching.

Down the hall.

He points left.

Only one door open. Mine.

It's not much bigger than a prison cell, doesn't look too different either. A single bed and a small desk against the wall. A bucket with a toilet seat on top as a makeshift prison toilet. Bars over the window and multiple locks on the door.

He's left a pair of joggers and a plain black t-shirt on the bed. A book on the Satipatthana Sutta.

Worlds better than what you had.

Still a prison though.

A prison and not a prison.

He comes up behind me, looks around the room as though seeing it through my eyes.

I figured I can let you out for a shower once or twice a week, but I need to sort out the door and window first.

So you can't escape.

And I'll bring you meals when I can manage or leave some stuff with you.

Alright. Thank you. This is all - well, I really appreciate it.

Yeah.

And hopefully he'll give me a kettle and I'll be able to make tea. Tea and a book. I never thought I'd experience those kinds of pleasures again.

Or you can throw the hot water on him, catch him off guard.

And that's why he won't give you one. He won't take the chance.

Not yet. But we have time.

Not enough.

Well, I'll leave you to it. But I'll be back this evening sometime.

Alright. Thanks.

He nods, pulls the door closed, and locks at least three locks. Deadbolt. Latch. Another bolt into the frame.

No escape. The bars on the window solid. Inside and out.

The view's nice though. Any view is nice. A modest patch of yard and fence with bushes, a couple of trees. Must be the back of the house. Doesn't look like London. And it's too quiet out there. Maybe somewhere rural. No hope of signalling anyone from here.

Although of course he's already thought it all through. Thought with my mind, my desperation to get away, all the clever and violent ways out.

One day he'll slip.

Maybe.

I change into my joggers and t-shirt. No underwear or socks. Sit on the bed and look about the room. My room.

It's peaceful. The colours and shapes. The daylight washing the wall. The duvet is soft. I caress it with my fingertips. But nothing as alluring as the window. What's beyond it. If I could just break into small, ephemeral pieces, I could slip through the bars, drift off into the wind and the world beyond.

Be grateful for what you've got.

I lie back, stare up at the ceiling. The rough triangle of light. Get under the covers and pull them up to my chin.

It's okay. We're safe. It's okay.

Still trapped. Can't be trapped here.

He'll slip. I have to believe he'll slip. And then, nothing will be able to hold me back.

But until then, rest. Be. You won't get closer to it by thinking about it.

And we have the book. That was nice of him. Has he read it? Hopefully. I can read it slowly, consider each line. Meditate on the words. It'll be just like back at the monastery.

If you want it to be. It's all in your mind anyway.

Maybe.

The knock wakes me. And then it's click-click-click as he opens the door's many locks, pushes it slowly in. He jostles a full carrier bag past the doorframe and sets it down on my desk.

Got you some extra supplies. I'm going away for a few days, so there should be enough to last you until I'm back.

Okay. Thanks.

I get up, and he takes a step backwards to keep his distance. In the bag there's digestive biscuits, Pringles, breakfast bars, a couple of reduced sandwiches.

My stomach kicks. All the flavours and textures on my tongue. It'd fill my belly properly for the first time since I woke here.

He lingers in the doorway, watching me.

I've just put a pizza in. You fancy joining me for a beer?

What, downstairs?

Yeah. Just for a little while.

Do it. Do it.

Yeah, sure. Sounds good. Now?

Sure, come on.

He walks ahead, keeps glancing back so I can't try anything, push him down the stairs or run up and get a choke on him.

Through the hallway. Obviously he'll have all the doors and windows locked. That won't be an option.

Into the living room. He gestures me into the armchair.

Wait there.

The TV's on. BBC News. Talking about help for the struggling West End.

The room's tidier than I was expecting. Quite nicely furnished. Maybe out there, he's actually quite respectable and normal. Only I know the darkness inside him.

Inside you both.

Take it to your grave.

People being fined for being caught in each other's houses. Police patrolling the empty streets. Nationwide lockdown. Death toll at a new record.

He stops in the doorway, a can of beer in each hand.

What's all this?

Here.

He hands me a beer, finds the remote, switches channels to a football talk show.

What the fuck was that?

I didn't mean for you to find out that way. Or at all actually. I shouldn't have left the news on. Don't worry about it. It doesn't affect you.

What happened?

He drinks his beer. Lights a cigarette, offers me one.

There was a virus that broke out in China last year.

Respiratory virus. No one expected it to be so bad, so they weren't prepared for it. Killed a bunch of older folks and people with pre-existing health conditions, you know. Overwhelmed the health services so the government put everyone under lockdown. Pretty much no one can work or go anywhere. Not just here. It's pretty much all over the world.

He's fucking with me. He timed it perfectly so I'd see the news report. Where did he get it? Some YouTube prank video?

He reads my disbelief but doesn't react.

What if it is true? The world out there I've been longing for all this time has broken down. Is Mum okay? She'd have been in the epicentre of it at work. Maybe it took her out. And even if I did escape, I'd be confined to a prison not much different than this one. Varying stages of freedom, but never the real thing.

Why bother trying?

But that's what he wants you to think. He wants you all sedate and Stockholm Syndromed. It'd suit him just fine for you to think the world was destroyed out there and it was in your best interests to stay trapped in your prison.

No prison but a psychological one. If he had control of my mind, he wouldn't need bars on the window or locks on the door. But he'd keep them for good measure.

He gets off on the control. Feeling like a God. But the wrong kind of god.

Can we watch the news?

Better not. I'll get you a newspaper if you really want to know, but like I said, it doesn't affect you. Just a political shitshow.

His phone alarm goes, and he fetches the pizza from the oven. Offers me a piece. It's still too hot, but I chew quickly, mouth overwhelmed by the rich flavours of a past life. It's only pizza. Warming my belly. But now it's gone. Wash it down with beer. Was it only the one piece? I don't want to assume. Don't want to piss him off by overstepping my bounds. It's nice enough of him to share. He could have eaten it all by himself with me watching.

Onscreen, the panel members analyse the latest goal attempts from some Premier League team. Drawing coloured arrows and talking player positioning and pass timings.

He eats two slices. Gestures me as he takes a third.

Thanks.

It's good. Warm and the taste of the cheese and tomato and the pepperoni. But the pleasure already less than the first slice. You build it up in your mind, but it's just a slice of pizza. Just a bed. Just a book with words on it.

You could put me back in a life of luxury, of hot tubs and balconies and takeaway meals every night, and I'd still be black and miserable.

It's a bit late for that, isn't it?

Monastic life changed you, and this changed you again.

Just a product of environment.

But I deserve more. There has to be more to look forward to. To keep me sane.

And that's your problem.

Always going to suffer for it.

But who is here to suffer anymore? There is suffering out there, but where could it possibly land? Pain and discomfort but never dukkha.

He finishes the last of the pizza, drinks his beer, and burps. Puts his feet up and watches the show.

I drink. Getting towards the end. Will he give me a second one? I wouldn't mind a second. Especially with the pizza to wash it down and all my food upstairs. Although can't eat that all at once. Need to ration it out. But maybe a few biscuits when I get back. Biscuits and a little read of the book. All that's missing is the tea. And then I'll fall asleep in my soft bed, watching the garden in the moonlight if there's any.

Bliss even in this prison.

But doesn't bliss always end with suffering? Maybe a

different kind of bliss.

Don't cling to these meaningless things. It's okay to enjoy them, but don't mourn them. All impermanent, you know. Gone before you could even attempt to hold them.

He goes for another beer, hands me a second.

Thanks man.

It's alright.

He settles back, drinks, gets out another cigarette and tries to light it. Click click click. But it doesn't light. Click click.

Fucking thing.

Click click.

He puts it away and gets to his feet. Stay there. Goes out of view. The sound of him on the stairs going up.

Now. It has to be now, Sam.

The kitchen. Quickly. Carefully. On the balls of your feet. He's up on the landing. Okay, into the kitchen. Try the drawers. Something sharp. Only cutlery. The other one. Wooden spoons and spatulas. A rolling pin. No. It has to be sharp. Quickly, Sam. The other drawer. It's no good. He won't have left knives lying around. They'll be locked away somewhere.

No. Here in the drawer, chef knives, a bread knife, steak knives, couple of paring knives.

Footsteps.

Go.

I take the paring knife and hold it against my leg, out of view, slip back into the living room.

He's coming. Quick. Need to hide it. Just in the waistband of your joggers. On your right side. Hide it with the t-shirt.

His figure blocks the hallway light and he comes back to his seat, lights up a cigarette. Doesn't offer me one.

Try to sit still. Look calm. Like nothing happened. Need to wait for the right moment. Not now. Not here.

Then when? When his back is turned? Going upstairs? Can't wait too long or he'll notice the missing knife.

He'll be away for a few days. Better do it before. Otherwise you'll think your way out of it.

Shut up. Just forget about it. Drink the beer. Watch the show. Watch the breath. Don't give yourself away.

Well I'm probably going to hit the sack soon. I'll take you back.

Okay. Thanks. For this. It was nice.

Yeah. Maybe we can do something again one time when I'm back.

Alright, yeah.

He gets up, walks to the door, looks back, walks to the stairs, looks back.

I walk calmly, arms at my sides. Only inches away from it.

He goes up the steps, doesn't look back this time, keeps going.

Now. Nownownow. Hesitate just a second before the programming takes over. Execute order. Lift up my shirt and take out the knife, jump up an extra stair to close the distance.

He turns as I thrust the knife at him. It goes in, but he takes most of the strength out of it. Shouldn't have hesitated.

Pushes me back. Almost lose balance. The knife out again.

You fucking prick. Give me that.

Fuck you.

I slice the air in front of him and when he puts his arms up to protect himself he leaves his belly unprotected and I stick the knife in it.

Fuck you fuck you fuck you.

All the shit you've put me through, all this suffering, but never again. Never again.

Stab him again and again until he stops fighting and leans forward. I can't push his weight back, used all my gas on the kill. He slumps onto me. I try to direct his weight towards the wall, but he still knocks me down. Rolls over me. I roll too, catch myself before the end. His body slaps the laminate flooring and lies there. Blood pooling around him. Slowly. Graciously. In no real rush to leave his body but leaving whether he likes it or not.

It's over.

Not yet. Need to get the fuck out of this place.

Exhausted. Need to rest first.

No. Find the keys. He might have them on him. If not, somewhere in the house.

I roll him over, eyes unmoving but looking still for something, knife sticking out his side, feel his pockets. Find his phone, cigarettes, wallet, keys. Take them to the front door. There's a Yale lock I get open, but the door still won't open. Need a key for the deadlock. It could only be one of these two. The first fits in the lock but doesn't turn. The second won't even fit.

Fuck. He must have it hidden somewhere.

Hey, where's the fucking key man? I know you're still in there. Where's the fucking key?

But he doesn't even seem to be breathing anymore. I'm getting bloody staying here.

I sit on the bottom step to catch my breath for a second. Light a cigarette. Check his phone. I can't get into it without his passcode or biometrics, but I could make an emergency call.

And say what? That's not going to end well. Just focus on getting out of here.

Inhale. Exhale.

Okay, come on. Up the stairs. This room must be his. Nothing in his bedside drawers, in the dresser. Must be a safe somewhere.

Just smash a window. Toss a mattress out and jump. The door isn't the only way out.

It'd look more suspicious though. Your prints are already all over the knife, probably his body too. You need to think about your future on the other side of that door.

People will ask questions. I need my story straight. Can't end up in another prison.

Never mind the story. We can work that out on the way. First we need to get rid of the body and get out.

Should burn this place to the ground. But that would draw firemen. Cops. And even then, the basement would probably still be there, holding space for my inevitable return.

Fuck that. I'll put him there. Lock him in. It'd take a lot of effort to get to him. And who would bother?

I check his pockets again to make sure there's no other key. Feel around his dick in case there's something hidden there. Bastard.

I drag him across the floor to the basement stairs, smearing blood on the way. Give him a big shove and he rolls, rolls down the stairs and hits the door at the bottom. I walk slowly down, open the door, and drag his body to the wall where the cuff still lies. Look at him there in my place for a second, then leave him and lock the door behind me.

Okay, just wipe up the blood. Now it looks fine. Everything's in order. No one will know a thing.

Now get out. Probably have to smash a window, but scout the place first. Wait. Try the keys again. The one that fit. It moves a little in the lock but doesn't turn. Not to the left, but it turns right. The wrong way. The deadlock clicks as it withdraws from the frame.

Turn the handle and pull the door in. Cool air and evening sun.

Freedom.

It can't be. It doesn't make sense. I thought I'd die here.

So the breeze in the hairs on your arms is a lie? The clouds in the sky and the faint suggestion of a bird call?

If it is a lie, I don't want to know.

Get the fuck away from here and don't ever look back.

I close the door behind me, go to the end of the drive, turn left, and walk. Keep walking.

It doesn't matter where.

I'm probably going to hit the sack soon. I'll take you back.

Okay. Thanks. For this. It was nice.

Yeah. Maybe we can do something again one time when I'm back.

Alright, yeah.

He gets up, walks to the door, looks back, walks to the stairs, looks back.

I walk calmly, arms at my sides. Only inches away from the blade.

He goes up the steps, doesn't look back this time, keeps going.

He doesn't know. Just stay calm, and he won't know.

Down the corridor. He opens the door and stands back.

My arm covering any slight bulge in my clothes.

Thanks.

No problem. Goodnight, Sam.

Goodnight.

He shuts the door, locks me in. I wait for the sound of his footsteps to die, then take out the paring knife. Run my thumb along it. Sharp enough.

It'll do the job.

Is this really what you want?

No time to think about it. It's already done and decided. Just the doing of it left.

There's no rush. We have time to be for a minute. Get my mind in order.

In order? Haha good luck with that.

You've wasted your life doing that. What's another few hours?

Wait until he's gone at least.

Could take a nap. And if he's away, it doesn't have to be today.

What, give yourself time to try and rationalise your way out of it? You're being stupid. You waited so long for this chance and now you're going to fuck about?

Shut up. Just shut up for a minute.

I put it under the pillow, go in the carrier bag, take out the rich tea biscuits. Eat one. Another. Pace the room with light steps so he won't hear. Still listening for any footsteps or doors opening and closing.

Should read some suttas. For the road.

More intellectualising.

Or at least meditate. I want to be mindful when I go.

Fine, then meditate. Better than cramming your face with food.

Is it? This close to the end, what does it really matter?

I place the pillow on the ground, sit cross-legged with the knife on the carpet under my legs. Hands together and eyes closed. The darkness the only thing I'll ever know.

Hahaha. Even now, you're full of shit. You think death is darkness? This isn't the end. This is only the beginning. The awakening from the dream.

But I'm scared.

No, you're not. Who is here to be scared?

Okay, fine then. Fear is present here.

Yes, but fear is not a problem.

Come back to the breath, Sam. Back to where you always start.

Come home.

Inhale.

Exhale.

Inhale.

Exhale.

A little pain and then it's all over. And what is pain to you anymore?

Only a sensation like the breath or music or a foul smell. You've felt pain far beyond this.

But it's what the pain means.

And what does it mean?

The end. The end of me as I know myself. The energy of the universe will metamorphose and my energy will be recycled, my spirit will live on in collective consciousness, but Sam here will die. Nothing can change that.

I told you you'd only try to intellectualise it.

The breath, Sam. Drop back.

Inhale.

Exhale.

Inhale.

No time like the present. May as well get it over with.

No, please. Just a little longer. I'm not calm yet.

Will you ever be calm? Who says you're supposed to be?

No. It's true.

Touch the knife handle beneath my legs, grip it.

Here is power. As was known since the first man used a sharpened stone to kill his brother. Here is life and death.

A violent tremor shakes my body.

Put it down. The game's over. You're not going to use that thing on yourself. Only on him.

Not even him.

I put the knife down, pick it back up again.

Forget him. You know he won't go out without a fight.

But it's now, Sam. Push the thoughts from your head and ignore your body. It doesn't know what's good for it. Stuck in some ancient programming.

Hold my arm out. The faint green vein tracing up my wrist.

Do it. Doitdoitdoitdoit.

I push the point into my vein, drag the blade down its path. Harder. Deeper. You won't do it like that. The cold sensation but no pain. Blood leaking. Keep going, Sam. You're doing well. Keep going.

Now the pain stinging as a second phantom knife cuts along the line.

And the other one. Best to be safe.

Not again.

You have to, Sam. Come on, one more, and then it's all over.

I transfer the knife to my left hand, already wet with blood. Follow the line. Join the dots. Just like a kid. Nearly done. You've already done it.

And rest. Just breathe.

Knife falls away, and I hold my hands in my lap as the blood runs. Straighten my back and close my eyes.

Pain painpainpainpain. Pain with warmth. Endogenous opioids. Even now my body trying to numb itself.

My legs wet with blood. Pooling in my lap.

Need to be sick.

Just breathe. Watch the breath.

While you still can.

Inhale. Exhale. Inhaleexhale.

In another room in another world, locks click and another man runs in, kicks the knife away, presses a towel to your arms. Stems the bleeding. And you wake up in the basement. Or here. Or anywhere. Does it really matter?

Just thoughts. Let them pass. They're as lost as you.

Think of what's to come. So much of it is beautiful.

All this here doesn't matter. Insignificant to the universe.

But not to me.

Even now, you hold on. Even now if you could go back and do it all again, you would. Just for the sake of being.

I would.

So dizzy, with eyes open or closed.

Take me now. Please. I've suffered enough.

Inhale. Exhale.

Feel the blood running down. Slowly now. Time slowing. What is time? The body and mind shutting down as the energy drains away.

Inhale.

Exhale.

Inhale…

Buddhist Terminology

Ajahn – 'Teacher', used as an honorific in the Thai Forest Tradition for senior Buddhist monks.

Anicca – 'Impermanence', one of the Buddha's three marks of existence, along with dukkha and anattā (non-self).

Bhikkhu - Refers to ordained monks but also more broadly, to anyone on the path of enlightenment.

Bodhisatta (English/Sanskrit: Bodhisattva) – A being who has achieved enlightenment but returned, so to speak, as the Buddha did, to aid the unenlightened on the path. Also refers to those who have committed to Buddhahood and are still on the journey.

Dhamma – Roughly translated as 'law', 'duty', or 'nature', dhamma refers to the Buddha's teachings, the natural law of being, and the embodiment of spiritual truth.

Dukkha - Roughly translated as 'suffering', 'dissatisfaction', or 'dis-ease', dukkha refers not so much to physical pain or unpleasant thought but to the spiritual discontent or psychological pain caused by delusion and ignorance and attachment to ideas of self and permanence. It is the foundation of the Buddha's four noble truths. The end of dukkha is nibbāna (nirvana).

Kamma (English/ Sanskrit: Karma) - Refers to the law of cause and effect in the world, both individual and collective. More than the simple conception of divine retribution in the Western usage of the word. Kamma is the natural consequence of prior conditions and all of its manifestations.

Karuṇā – Roughly 'compassion'.

Mara – The demon who tried to coerce the Buddha away from enlightenment as he sat under the Bodhi tree. Mara embodies the intoxicating influence of the world and the antithesis of awakening.

Mettā – Loving kindness. A type of meditation used to channel compassion and good will for all beings.

Nibbāna (English: Nirvana) – A state of non-clinging, liberation from dukkha and samsara, although at the same time, coexisting with samsara. Individuals can reach a state wherein they are permanently in nibbāna, synonymous with enlightenment or Buddhahood.

Samsāra (English: Samsara) – Refers to rebirth and cyclical existence, ordinary worldly existence which can be a source of such suffering at times, but is necessary and ultimately supports even nirvana.

Sangha - Roughly translated as 'community', sangha refers both to the general community of those on the path of enlightenment and the individual community within a given monastery or Buddhist centre.

Sati - A state of concentration in Buddhism, commonly translated as 'mindfulness'. It forms the basis of vipassanā, 'insight' meditation.

Sutta (English/Sanskrit: Sutra) – Refers more generally to ancient Indian script, but also specifically to the canonical scriptures in Buddhism taken as records of the Buddha's teachings.

Printed in Great Britain
by Amazon